Faking It With My Enemy

A BILLIONAIRE AGE GAP ROMANCE

H.J. FLORIS

Contents

CHAPTER ONE

Iris

I stare at Carl, shocked to my core by what I'm hearing from him.

"You're breaking up with *me*?" I ask.

Carl, my six-foot-one boyfriend, or ex, with a mop of perfectly mixed blonde and brown hair and a smile so beautiful it's feminine, nods his head solemnly. His brown eyes stare at me with...is that *pity?*

"I'm sorry, Iris, it's just the way it needs to be. We are too different; we wouldn't have worked out in the long run."

My eyes narrow. Is this fucker really spewing cliché excuses at me right now? Lightening cracks right above us, the wind picks up, and people rush past us on the sidewalk, trying to get to wherever they are going to before the rain starts.

But I stay rooted to the spot. This shock I'm feeling right now is not due to the heartbreak from being dumped by Carl. I don't really love him. I do like him, and have affection for him, but I don't feel that deep type of love that would have caused me to hyperventilate after he said what he just said. I'm usually smarter than this. I don't date jerks like Carl. But I met him a few weeks after I moved to New York, and he had played all the right tunes with me. A couple months into the relationship, I had known Carl wasn't a catch. Why had I stayed with him still? Let's call it...riding that New York high. And now, a year and six months after the fact, walking home from a restaurant—after a meal that Carl was too cheap to pay for—and freezing from the cold in my silk shirt, Carl does what I didn't have the balls to do.

I snicker at the annoyance of it all. I look at him, huddled in his jacket, his hair somehow remaining perfect even in the whirling wind. Jerk.

"You couldn't have waited till we got to my place? Huh, Carl? You couldn't have waited."

He shrugs. "I can't keep pretending anymore, I guess. It's not you, it's me."

I cannot believe my ears. Now he's just dropping lines straight from T.V. rom-coms. I suddenly hate myself so much right now. How could I have dated this ass for a full year and a half?

I look up at the night sky; the clouds are already heavy with the rain they are about to pour down. More people rush past us, still in a hurry to get to wherever they're going. Wise choice. Just then, droplets of rain start to fall. I need to stop being stupid from this moment on. Carl, my dumbest decision as of right now, is apparently now out of my life. I need to start making smart choices, and my first smart choice would be to get out of this rain that promises to be a pisser and head home.

I look back at Carl and scoff. I can't even. My back to the street, I walk to the edge of the walkway, to hail a cab. And because my back is to the street, I don't see the puddle of water already gathered by the side of the road. I slip, and my arms flail out as I get propelled toward the busy road. Someone screams as a car comes straight at me. I stare in shock for the second time tonight, but this time, I stare directly into bright headlights.

My mind blanks at the worst possible time. And then, I am yanked back to the walkway. The car that was going to flatten me seconds ago speeds past, with the driver yelling *'Asshole!'* My heart starts beating again. I look up into the eyes of my saviour, and I find myself staring into Carl's brown eyes. And just like that, my relief at being saved turns to annoyance.

I jerk my arms away from his grip. A car horn blares and forces both of us to turn to look. There's a cab waiting by the side of the road. So I had gotten a cab after all. I start to walk toward it, but a startled gasp leaves my mouth as Carl pushes me aside to get to the cab first.

"What the hell?"

I stand on the sidewalk, stupefied, as Carl gets into the cab.

"You're welcome," Carl says, just as the cab glides into the road and zooms away.

At that moment, the sky opens up, and rain starts falling in large wet drops.

"Son of a bitch!" I shout at the sky.

***

Asshole! No, no, no, asswipe. Yeah, *asswipe* is a more suited word for him. The pathetic excuse for a man I can't believe I actually dated. The man that just broke up with me on a *sidewalk*, and then steals my cab right after. I almost lost my life just now, and this *asswipe* takes my cab? Who does that?

Asshole is the preferable part for some people in sex, so even asshole's got some weight. But nothing could be lower than a thing used to wipe the ass itself, right? So, yeah, *asswipe* is definitely more suitable.

These thoughts run through my head as I climb up the stairs of the office building. I am dripping water on the stairs with every step I take. I don't know this office building—I never do really—and I don't know what the workers in this building do, but this is something I do sometimes. When I get aggravated to the point where I want to scream, I go to a roof of a really tall building. Tall buildings are probably my favorite things about New York.

With everything that just happened to me, I'll say this scenario calls for a good scream. I climb—no, I march—up the stairs, which I hope lead me to a roof. I get to the end of the stairs see a door in front of me. I push it, and it opens with a jerk because of the force of my hand. I march forward as eyes start to adjust to my surroundings.

The roof is a wide spread of space and clean too. Perfect. The raindrops meet the floor in splashes, adding to the puddle of water already formed on the floor. I close my eyes and let the rain beat on me. It's so cold, and maybe there's a part of me that hopes the cold will somehow numb the rage in me. Life goes on below me, on the busy street of New York. But, for that second, life stops for me.

I feel a calmness in me, but I don't let it settle. I am a woman with a mission, a mission to curse my ex into oblivion, and I am not going to be swayed. Not even by a feeling of peace. I move forward till I get to the railing surrounding the roof. I grip it with my hands and try to shake it. It stays sturdy. Fucking Carl is *not* going to be the death of me. Satisfied, I grip the railing and scream.

The scream's not a sissy one; it's a really loud one because when I put my mind to something, I really go for it. But it gets drowned in the patter of raindrops meeting the ground.

"You are an asswipe, Carl Lingstrom. You don't even deserve to be called an ass. That's an insult to asses all over the world. You're an *asswipe*. You asshole!"

I know I'm contradicting myself right now, but I don't care. I'm soaking wet, my hair is dripping, and my shirt is plastered to my body like another skin. I walk a few feet away from the railing and pace back and forth, and then I go back to the railing.

"You are the most pathetic waste of space human being I have ever met. Your dick is shrivelled, and your hair is a jaded version of Justin Bieber!"

Of course, that last sentence is the opposite in truth, but I am hitting him where it hurts. I know Carl, and oh yeah, this would hurt. Light bulb moment. I should record this. I root in my pocket for my phone, and then almost drop it as I hear a voice behind me.

"Wow, colourful," the voice says.

I turn slowly toward the sound of the voice. In all my years of climbing up roofs of buildings I don't know, I have never met another soul. The voice stays in the shadows, under a roof extension that also covers a table on which sits a flower pot. I squint, trying to see the owner of the voice, but the dark, plus the rain drops falling on my face, make it hard. But the lights from surrounding buildings help me make an outline.

He is tall, about a head taller than I am. His hands are in the pockets of his trousers, and I can see the outline of his impressively muscled arms even from where I'm standing. His shirt sleeves are rolled up to his elbows, and his broad chest stretches the fabric of his white shirt so tight, spandex would be jealous. I frown, because hot or not—and this guy was definitely hitting the hot-o-meter out of the park—he is still interrupting my cursing session.

"Who are you?" I ask rudely, not even bothering to hide my irritation.

"I think that question should be mine to ask. Who are *you*?"

He stands up, and I realize he was leaning against the table all the while. And with that realization, I see he is a little bit taller than I had originally thought. I squint my eyes more, trying to figure out who I am speaking to. And for some reason, that annoys me even more.

"Look, hotshot, I don't have the time to play smartass with you, so why don't you—"

"Right, cause you're so busy thinking of colourful insults for your boyfriend," he says dryly, cutting me off.

"He is not my boyfriend," I say through gritted teeth. I fold my arms together. I don't know why I'm clarifying this to this...annoying stranger, or why it's even suddenly so important to me. And I am cold. So cold. My silk shirt is really flimsy, and the cold is penetrating me with no buffer whatsoever.

He nods, once.

"Ah. Not your boyfriend. Okay, got it. But how do you know if his dick is shrivelled or not then?"

I swear I can actually feel the steam spouting out of my ears. Thunder cracks above us. Neither of us flinch.

"Who. The. Hell. Are. You," I ask again.

"I'm the owner of this building," he says.

I stare at him for a couple of seconds. Lightning streaks across the sky, and it illuminates his face for a bit. Just a second, really, but in that second, I get the full effect of the man standing in front of me. Poise. Beauty. Power. Those are my immediate feelings that come to mind when I see his face. He isn't rugged. That word is too rough for the manicured finery of his person. But he is definitely not soft either. His body and face possess hard planes. His jawline is firm, his cheekbones are high and hard. His mouth, furnished with lips that look designed for kissing, is stretched into a thin, disapproving line. And his eyes, sharp and piercing, are focused on me. Even in the black night, they possess their own mysterious darkness. I shiver, and I'm not sure if it's because of the rain or those eyes.

"This place is not for cursing at exes, so, whatever your drama is with this asswipe character, I suggest you take it home."

I curl my lips into a sneer. "Or what?"

His eyebrows tilt. He is obviously surprised by my audacity.

"Or I call security," he says.

CHAPTER TWO

Dayton

I watch as her eyes narrow to slits in disbelief.

"*Excuse me?*"

She draws out the words, her voice coming out in what almost sounds like a squeak.

I sometimes like to come up to the roof and for one sole reason, the peace and quiet. It is literally the only place that guarantees it. Also, I was here to think about the idea Karen, my head of PR and a woman who knows her job pretty well, had suggested earlier to me today. I had been on the roof for about thirty minutes when this woman came barging in on me. And now, she has taken away my peace and quiet with her interruption.

I take in her defiant pose. Her arms are crossed over her chest; her eyes are flashing with a mixture of shock and annoyance. Her black hair is dripping wet from the rain falling on her. Her shirt, a flimsy rayon top no sane person should be wearing in the rain, sticks to her body. It shouldn't be surprising though. From the little I've garnered from her little show tonight, I think sanity is the least of her priorities. She stands more than a head shorter than me, but that doesn't stop her from giving me the stink eye. Strangely, that amuses me for some reason.

"You heard me. I can have security here before you can even blink. You want to go that way? Or you want to just quietly leave on your own right now?" I ask, giving her a choice. Which is being fair, in my own opinion.

I didn't think her head could tilt even higher than it already did, but apparently it can, as she angles it even higher.

"In case you've forgotten, this is America. We pride ourselves in our freedom here. You can't just take me off the roof."

The rain is now a slight drizzle, but she's still shivering badly from the cold. That isn't my main concern right now though.

"Actually, I can. This is private property, *my* property, and I can do whatever the hell I want. I don't want some loud woman screaming obscenities on my roof. I want her off."

Her eyebrows jump. "Loud? I'll show you loud."

She turns on her heels and grips the railing again.

"Men are assholes. All men should die," she screams into the night sky.

I don't even know it's going to happen until a chuckle bursts out of me.

"You get points for trying," I murmur to myself even as I bring out my phone from my pocket. I dial a number and listen as it rings once and is picked up on the other end.

"Max, yes, I have a situation here," I say into the phone. I get confirmation and drop the call.

I fold my arms across my chest and lean back again to watch the show. She has now turned back to face me, her pose mirroring mine. Her chest heaves from the effort her screaming exercise had taken. I find myself stirred by the sight of her, with her standing a few feet away from me, dripping wet. Her clinging, drenched shirt leaves me with no obfuscation to the streamline of her shapely body. Her breasts heave with every breath, and the stubborn notch of her nipples through her bra tempt me to stare. Her tight-fit trousers cling even more to her slender limbs, and even though she's a head shorter than me, her legs seem to go on for miles. Her feet are in a pair of shoes that don't quite look like heels, but are not flat either. There's a nomenclature for her footwear, but I'm not conversant with female clothes. Her handbag, a shiny black bag, is on the floor beside the railing, where she had dropped it when she came onto the roof.

My eyes track back to her face. I'm no artist, but I get this feeling that a painting of her face would catch my attention. Even more, I would buy it. That is how striking she looks. Her hair, sodden by the rain, frames her face. Her eyes, a pair of glittering black, continue to stare daggers at me, her eyebrows curved in a defiant arch over them.

My gaze is jerked from staring at her when Max, my head of security, and the new guy on duty with him, walk onto the roof. Max, a fit and burly man with the same height as me and facial expression smoothed into a blank stare, gives me a small nod. His gaze tracks over to the woman and back to me.

"Mr. Pade," he says, his voice showing no hint of what he's thinking.

"Please, escort this young woman off the building," I say.

Max and his partner give me slight nods and walk over to the woman.

"Ma'am, please, we'd like you to come with us," Max says, his voice low as he points toward the door. His partner picks up her bag from the floor and waits for her to comply.

She looks at Max, and then at his partner, and then she focuses those laser eyes on me. Weirdly again, her rage gives me some sick pleasure. I curl my lips into a tiny smirk, and, oh, she sees it. Her eyes narrow to slits again as she stares daggers into me. If looks could kill....

"You're an asshole," she mutters to me, rage evident in every word.

She starts to stomp off toward the door; Max's partner follows her with her bag.

"Make sure she gets into a cab," I say to Max.

"Okay, Mr. Pade," he replies as he leads her down.

The door closes behind them and, save for the soft patter of dropping rain, there is no more disturbance. I lean against the table to savour the peace once again. And I find myself missing the noise.

For some inexplicable reason, that annoys me. I walk to the door on the roof and open it. I walk down the short flight of stairs to my office. The fruity sweet scent of my office's air freshener welcomes me, and I stroll across the tiled floors to the glass walls that offer a view of the street down below me. I see the woman, Max, and his partner standing on the sidewalk. I watch as Max's partner says something to the woman and she shakes her head. She runs a hand through her hair, clearly agitated now. Max's jacket is now around her shoulders. I take out my phone and dial the company's security number again. I watch as Max answers the call.

"What's going on down there, Max?" I ask.

Max turns his back on the woman and his partner and walks a few feet away from them.

"Sir, the woman can't seem to find her purse, and she claims her money and credit cards are in it. Her cellphone is dead too, sir. There is no way to pay for a cab if she calls one."

I watch the woman's distant figure. She's pacing back and forth; she's clearly in distress. I draw my phone away from my ear to look at the time; it's half past eleven. I look down at her again.

"I'm coming down," I say and cut the call.

I pick my suit jacket up from the sofa where I had put it earlier. Seconds later, I join them on the sidewalk. Despite the rain, the street is still busy, and soft music continues to filter out from open bars and pubs close by. The wind blows cold as the rain is now reduced to an even lighter drizzle. I look at her. She's staring at me, and even though I can almost see her teeth chattering from the cold, she still manages to give me that murdering look. Strangely, I feel my lips starting to curve at the sight of it.

I look at Max. "I'll take care of this."

Max nods and turns to her. She takes off his jacket, and I watch her face soften as she smiles up at him.

"Thank you," she says to him, as she hands him his jacket.

"You're welcome, ma'am," Max replies, and with another succinct nod at me, he turns and leaves.

Even as I drape my jacket around her shoulders, I watch in strangely amusing surprise as her face frosts over again. Her spine stiffens, and I can almost hear it snap into place.

"Come on, I'll give you a ride home." I place my hand on her upper back to guide her to my car parked by the sidewalk. She jerks slightly at the contact then she springs forward, creating distance between us.

"I don't need your help," she says, ice in her voice.

I don't stop walking. I push her back again, this time applying a little bit more pressure. I give her no choice but to keep on walking too, even though she clearly doesn't want to. We soon get to my car and I open the door. I look back at her.

"You know you do. It looks like the rain is picking up again; you don't want to be caught up in it a second time. You want to catch pneumonia?" I ask, with enough derision in my voice for her to clearly hear.

She does, and her eyes flash with anger as she looks up at me. It surprises me how much I enjoy that look in her eyes, for some reason I don't even know. She doesn't get in, and we stay like this for a minute, staring at each other. The light drizzle picks up slightly. She flinches, her raised chin drops, and she finally gets in. I close the door and smirk as I walk to the other side of the car. I get in and start the car. She sits just as stiffly as she had stood on the sidewalk.

"Address?"

"345 Holby Drive."

Her response is stiff, and she remains silent as I start to drive. The rain drops in full torrents again, the droplets hitting the windshield of the car in fat splats. It's midnight so traffic is understandably light.

"You can charge your phone," I offer.

She looks down at the charging port then back at me. I see her struggling with the need to charge her phone and her desire to hold on to her hatred for me. She obviously decides she can do both as she takes out her charger and plugs in her phone, all the while ignoring me. Her phone comes on and the screensaver picture of her and a man with blonde hair smiling into the camera flashes on the screen. She stares at the picture for a full minute, and with a calmness I haven't seen in her throughout the time I have known her, she changes the image to custom one of a German shepherd. Messages start to roll in, but she just ignores it all as she rests her head on her seat.

We drive the remaining way in silence, getting to her address ten minutes later. I pull over, and she opens her eyes. She looks at me, and the weariness in her eyes now is in marked contrast to the fire I had grown accustomed to seeing. I make sure my lips curl into a smirk as I look up at the apartment building I pulled up in front of and back at her.

"I'm surprised some people can bear to live with you given your intolerable loud ways."

And just like that, her eyes spark with annoyance, bringing that fire back. She unplugs her phone.

"Fuck you," she says.

She opens the door and gets out of the car, slamming the door with enough force I'm sure she hopes removes the door from its hinges. I watch her walk, no, stomp, up to the building. I smile, oddly pleased.

CHAPTER THREE

Iris

IRIS

I adjust the modifications to reduce the number of stripes on the gown I'm designing. This many stripes makes the gown look like the hides of two zebras mating on a rug. What a visual. I inflate the puffed sleeve a little more, giving it that haughty look. Because, yeah, this is a pretty smug gown.

I smile smugly to myself as I continue making adjustments on the tablet I use mostly for designing. It's been a week, roughly, since fucking Carl Lingstrom broke up with me. And, as I know—in a really honest part of my mind—Carl is not someone to lose sleep over. Really, he is not. He was not an abusive man, not physically and not mentally either. He didn't make me feel less of myself when I was with him. In fact, I felt fucking great about myself when I was with him. You know, you just look at him, at his ridiculously handsome face and his custom playboy hair, and you see that that was all he had. He takes really great care of his face and most especially his hair, enough in front of you, that you realize pretty soon that they were his tools. His only way to get what he wants in the world. And without them, he doesn't have the slightest clue what to do with himself.

So, you look at someone like that, and suddenly you feel great about yourself. Because you know you've got more than your looks going for you. You've got a hell of a brain and guts. Guts that guys like Carl could only ever dream of having.

But while Carl was not an abuser, of any sorts, he was a user. And really, what else was to be expected of a guy who always had to use what he had to get what he wants? *Using* is part of his DNA, his freaking genetic makeup. And it was for petty things too. I guess, at the core of it, that's what makes it even worse. He would use me to get into places like a favorite restaurant of his. Not that I am a BFD in New York, or something. And, thank God for that, as all you have to be to get into most of the restaurants here is a normal person. You know, normal, like have a credit card that can pay for whatever you order for. So you don't look over at your girlfriend—who is supposed to be enjoying a date with you—and ask for her credit card right in the middle of a meal.

Another instance of Carl being a user is somehow only having a girlfriend when it's comfortable. Like when he needs to impress his boss with how together his life is.

Carl is a salesman. A salesman, for God's sake.

Anyway, user aside, there was really nothing much to Carl to feel angered about. He was just a bad choice in a bad time. So that's why I'm not going to be losing any sleep over him. Anymore. I am going to be focused on my work, as my career in design is what's important. I have been in New York for a year and seven months now, give or take a week. And the plan is to work at dream fashion company, ENAMOURED, and impress them with the genius creativity of my designs. The ultimate plan is to make senior designer within a year at the firm.

Yeah, yeah, wild thinking. After taking a bite out of the Big Apple, I know that now. Senior designer in a year? Hmph. I'll be lucky if I ever get my designs out to the world in five. There are so many talented people here in New York. So many of them, I don't even begin to count. But I still gotta do the work I came here to do. And I've given Carl way too much of my time as it is.

I make another change to the gown on the tablet. This particular design is one of my originals. And a personal favorite of mine. I've always had a thing for stripes, most especially stripes that ebb and flow into miles and miles of material that pool at one's feet. And this gown has it all. I'm really excited to see where this design takes me. I'm doing this on my own time, and normally, I should be having lunch right now. Thinking of lunch, I take a bite out of the burger I had all but forgotten on the table beside me.

It says Junior Designer on my work form for ENAMOURED, but really all I do here is mostly non-design stuff. In fact, it's like I'm doing things that take me even farther away from presenting my designs every day. But sometimes, at least it's dignified, like running a senior designer's completed design through a design algorithm used exclusively by the company. And I get to write up the adjustments the algorithm makes, and sometimes even add my own suggestions. But then, other times, it's mind-numbing stuff like ordering design materials and tools online, and helping to set up a space for the company's mini design show every two weeks. On days like that, I get through the day by reminding myself over and over again why I moved to New York in the first place. And why I work for ENAMOURED.

I and six other junior designers share an office space on the third floor of the company's building, with each of us having our own workstation. Right now, the office is empty, except for me.

Somehow, my mind goes back to Carl, as unhealthy as that is. But then, even as Carl was undoubtedly an asshole in our relationship, there had been good times too. In the early months of our relationship, we had had fun. We had the most fun when we used to go visiting interesting spots all over New York. We were still mostly spending my money, but the moments were so interesting I didn't notice. Even after a couple months, when I had started to notice Carl's cheap pattern of somehow evading paying for most of the stuff we got, we still had fun.

I look up as Alyssa Penny, a fellow junior assistant and friend, walks into the office. Alyssa is a five-foot-four brunette with a beautiful lithe figure that probably makes her better suited to being a model than a designer. She is also my only true friend, and probably the only other designer in the office that I really respect.

Alyssa's honey-brown eyes are missing their usual playful sparkle. And her forehead is overrun with worry creases.

"What's wrong, Alyssa?" I ask.

When she just bites the corner of her lip and says nothing, I simply hold out my hand.

"Give me whatever you're hiding behind you. Come on, let's have it."

She looks at me for another minute before dropping the thing, which is a magazine, on my outstretched hand. I look down at the column Alyssa folded, and the fuzzy warmth of my memories with Carl disappears. On that page of the magazine is a picture of Carl, smiling, with a skimpily dressed model clutching tight to his left arm. The caption reads MAG COUPLE! and I feel sick to my stomach.

"I am so sorry, babe," Alyssa says, touching a hand to my shoulder.

I look up at her, having forgotten she was there.

Damn you, Carl.

***

I stare into my Manhattan drink, watching as the golden-brown liquid swirls gently. I know I'm on my way to drunk, tipsy at least. It's 9:00 p.m., a few miserable hours since I learned my ex is now dating a model. And not just any model.

My thoughts get interrupted as Brian, my friend and owner of the bar I'm in, walks up to me. I look up at him, his whiskey-brown eyes clouded with concern even as he smiles down at me softly.

"God, you're handsome," I say.

And he is, with his mop of thick brown hair sitting pretty on his head and framing his perfect face. His nose and lips are small and cute, fitting his soft dimpled cheeks, gentle chin, and brown eyes. His face is the kind of handsome that doesn't immediately arrest your attention but is impossible to forget. Impressive without being striking. He stands at least six feet tall. I can't tell how much over six feet he is.

He chuckles at my statement.

"Okay, I think you're ready to be cut off," he replies, his Irish accent coursing through.

I look down at my drink and shrug.

"Maybe. Yeah, probably."

I look up at him again, and that easy smile is still on his face.

"Why didn't I meet you first?" I ask wistfully.

I wasn't really expecting an answer, but Brian gives me one anyway.

"Because I was meant to be the friend that comforts you about him," he says.

Brian is a big believer of fate and things that are meant to be.

Me? I roll my eyes.

"I'd have preferred to have not met Carl in the first place, so I wouldn't have any reason to be comforted," I say, my words starting to slur a bit.

Brian chuckles again, and then he looks up. He smiles that easy smile again.

"Hey man," he says to somebody behind me.

I continue looking down into my drink, ignoring the person behind me. After a few seconds, I sigh deeply, my shoulders sagging with the effort. God, I hate Carl. Starting to go back into broody lane, I frown as I realize the person behind me hasn't taken a seat. And I can feel his or her gaze on me. I turn slowly on my seat till I'm looking up at him. Instant recognition slams into me as I see his face.

Crap.

CHAPTER FOUR

Dayton

"**C**rap," she says.

I feel my brows lift and watch as shock widens her eyes. She slaps a hand over her mouth.

"Did I just say that out loud?"

I feel the tension from the day drop away as I look at her. I nod, confirming her horror.

"Damn," she whispers to herself. She looks up at me. "I just can't seem to get it right with you, can I?"

My eyebrow jumps again. I slide easily onto the stool beside her. I don't remember her being this 'normal' from our first encounter. I raise my hand to signal a barman, but he is already heading toward me. He places a drink in front of me, a Manhattan, my usual.

"Thanks, Sven," I say.

I look up at Brian at the end of the bar. Brian, the owner of the bar, and my best friend, grins at me before returning his attention to the customer in front of him. After graduating from college with majors in Business Administration, I had gone into the corporate world, and Brian had gone on to open a pub. And he made a damn good pub owner. The success of *A ghrá* is testament to that fact.

I turn back to her, and I see that she is also nursing a Manhattan. She gives me a wry smile, raising her cup slightly. I smile back and take a sip of my drink. A live band belts out the lyrics to a song by an Irish singer, about bad loves and great sex, livening the pub with their music.

"Look, I'm sorry about the other day," she says, drawing my attention back to her. "I was having a really bad day, and I just wanted to scream. You got in the way of that. Sorry."

"You seem to be having a bad day today, too," I say, looking pointedly at her drink. "Feel like screaming?"

She looks down at her drink and chuckles lightly. She looks back up at me.

"No, not really," she says.

I nod.

"Okay, so, you only feel like screaming when your boyfriend dumps you," I say, making sure to add a biting tone to my sarcastic comment.

Her eyes flash with annoyance, that spark that had been missing. Seeing it excites me in ways I can't believe, starting a quickening in my groin. Suddenly, I feel better than I have in days.

"You jerk," she says. And to my dismay, tears fill her eyes. She doesn't let them drop though, and her voice turns to steel as she says, "See if I'll apologize to you again."

I shrug, ridiculously relieved she didn't cry.

"I wasn't looking for an apology. I needed space that night too. And I had gone up to the roof for it and for some quiet. And then you came up and got in *my* way. I was an ass to you too; you don't see me apologizing."

She seems to think about this for a minute. And then, she looks at me.

"Huh," she says after a minute. "That's true. You are not apologizing."

I shrug again. "I am not," I say. I take another sip of my Manhattan.

"Well, I am not sorry too then," she says.

"Fine by me."

She smiles. I look at her, and I see the sadness behind even that. I feel a tug on my heart at the sight of it. I wrap my fingers around my drink, because I suddenly feel the urge to run them through her hair.

"So, why are you not screaming tonight?" I ask.

"Because I'm more sad than mad, tonight," she says.

"Why?"

"You know how you're in a state of mind like, things aren't really all that good, I mean, they could be better, but they're still manageable?" she asks.

Before I can reply, she waves it off.

"You probably don't. With your important looking suit and expensive wristwatch," she looks me over. "Anyway," she sighs deeply, brooding into her drink. "I just hit rock bottom from even that, so..."

She sips her Manhattan and it's one of the saddest sips I've ever seen.

"You do know what they say about assumptions, right?"

She looks at me, her black eyes squinting at me.

"What do they say about them?"

"That you shouldn't make them," I say.

She snorts. "Yeah, right."

I let that go. "I do know what you mean. And it's not the feeling of hitting rock bottom that's making you sad. It's the thought of losing even that manageable bit of comfort," I add.

She looks at me, with interest now.

"I don't know. The manageable bit wasn't even all that," she says.

"Still," I say.

She is quiet for a minute, and then she shrugs, that sadness back in her eyes.

"Maybe," she murmurs.

I should go, I think to myself. I should just get up and leave right now. She's obviously a woman in a brooding mood, and I am no comforter. So, I should just up and leave right now. But even as I'm thinking this, I find words coming out of my mouth.

"Does this sad feeling happen to have anything to do with the asswipe ex?" I ask.

A short chuckle bursts out of her.

"You remember."

My lips curve in amusement.

"Can I ever forget?" I counter. "You literally screamed it out on my rooftop."

Now she laughs. "I did, didn't I?"

"It made for interesting viewing," I say, smiling as I recall the night in question.

"Oh yeah? You didn't seem to be interested that night," she says, looking over at me.

I hold her gaze.

"Oh, I was. I was interested," I say.

I watch, fascinated, as her pupils dilate just a fraction at my words, making her eyes even darker. And the knowledge that this is probably how her eyes are going to look like when she orgasms slams into me.

She swallows hard and breaks the eye contact.

Good thing, too, because I feel my heart pounding hard in my chest at the wayward thought that just ran through my mind.

I clear my throat. "So, you going to tell me what your being sad tonight has to do with your ex?" I ask.

She looks at me, her black eyes boring into mine. She opens her mouth to say something, but then she changes her mind.

"Do you want to get out of here?" she asks.

"To where?"

"I don't know," she answers.

Then when I think that's all, she adds, "Your place?"

Her eyes remain steady on mine, and I read the message in them loud and clear. I hold her gaze a while longer, to be sure she means what she is insinuating. Her eyes don't waver. She's serious, and who am I to say no?

"Let's go."

She stands as I do. I take her jacket from the back of her stool, placing it over her shoulders. I meet Brian's eyes for a second as I walk her out of the pub. I see surprise and something else I can't decipher. We walk out of the pub and into the busy street and windy night. I lead her to my parked car in front of the pub. We get in. Without saying a word, I pull away from the curb and onto the road. Traffic is light so the silence is pervasive. In the midst of all the brooding awkwardness, I realize I don't know her name.

"What's your name?" I ask.

She looks over at me jerkily; her eyes widen slightly with the implication of my question.

"Iris," she says quietly.

"Dayton," I offer, just as quietly.

We drive in silence for the rest of the journey. A few minutes later, I pull up in front of my penthouse building. I watch as her eyes widen at the gigantic block of glass walled flats, immersed steel pillars, and blinding lights. We get out, and I take her hand as we walk toward the entrance.

"Hey, Jake," I greet the doorman. The young lad with sandy brown hair and innocent stare smiles and nods. I throw my keys at him, which he catches expertly.

"Good evening, Mr. Pade," Jake murmurs. His gaze shifts to Iris. "Ma'am. I'll take care of your car, Mr. Pade," he says looking back toward me.

I nod to him and continue into the building with Iris. We walk to the elevator, and I punch in my penthouse number. We ride the elevator in silence. A few second later, it comes to a stop and opens into my house. We step in. I wonder what Iris thinks as she looks around.

"Can I get you a drink?" I ask.

Her gaze comes back to me.

"No," she says, her voice quiet.

I walk toward her, my gaze on her. She swallows.

"I don't usually do stuff like this," she says, then pauses. "But I just, I need..."

She trails off, her voice trembling on the last word. I do something I've been wanting to do ever since I saw her again in the pub. I slowly take her face between my hands.

"I know what you need," I say.

My gaze steady on hers, I slowly lower my lips to hers. I let my lips hover over hers a second before fusing our lips. The kiss is light, feathery and I simply take in her pulse as her lips part. I'm tempted to dive in but I don't; instead my mouth roams down to her throat as her pulse beats wildly against my skin. I pull back and stare in her eyes. The sadness is still there.

When I had said I knew what she needed, I had been talking about the sadness in her eyes. She needs me to help her forget it. So, I'll help her. Now as our mouths fuse again, there is only pleasure, pure and hot. I tear away her top, just as she yanks my shirt tucked in my pants. My hands interlock with her hands, stoking that hot pleasure until it burns. Our lips ravage each other until the glowing fire flares.

She arches as I release her bra, offering her perfectly round breasts to me. I latch on, sucking the gristly stub, at the same time lifting her up. She wraps tight around me as I carry her to my room. I lay her gently on the bed and join her. My lips go back to hers, giving. Her lips seek mine, taking. Our breaths quicken, our pulses trip. Smoothly, she slides out of her pants, I out of mine. I slide my fingers up her inner thigh and under her panties to find her wet, swollen, and ready. Yielding to temptation, I slip my fingers inside her, and she moans and clutches tighter to me. I push those fingers deeper, brushing them against her walls, and she shudders with the pleasure. And then I slide those panties all the way down. I take a condom from the bedside table and ease it over my hard and aching cock. Creeping back to her, I look into her eyes, eyes alight with libidinous excitement, and I drive inside her.

Our gazes remain locked as we move. And when I can't bear it anymore, I clasp my mouth to hers and immerse myself in her taste. But the feel of her tight and soaked grip on my shaft dominates my thoughts. She moans, and I know without asking that her sadness has faded to the far reaches of her mind. There is only pleasure, and it's overwhelming. She wraps her hands around my neck, and her legs wrap around my waist. Her lips peel off mine, and she moans against my chest. The pleasure yields in waves as we move, and the tide submerges me. I lift my head and stare down at her. Her lips are parted, her eyes are rolled back. Sweet thrills streak from our fusing sexes to my extremities. Ecstasy makes my toes coil and my breathing hitch. My climax approaches, and I fear its impact.

"Awww, I'm close," she whispers, and I grunt in agreement.

I'm close too, and I don't stop or slow down. I drive my shaft harder, deeper, burying myself in the delicious feel of her. Then I feel her constrict and tighten around me; her legs twitch and she cries out. Her sex's contortion around my cock trips my switch. My grunt is primal, marking the onset of my climax. I can't hold back, and my cock pumps hard, dumping a generous load into my sheath. I stay as I am, over her, for another minute, trying to catch my breath. And then I roll away. We don't say anything for a while, and the room is silent. She breaks the silence.

"Thank you," she whispers.

I look over at her; her eyes are closed, her cheeks flushed. I know why she's thanking me, but honestly, at this point, I feel pretty damn grateful to her too.

CHAPTER FIVE

Iris

I open my eyes slowly, squinting against the sunlight streaming into the room and on my face. I turn my head sideways and the knowledge that I am in a strange bed hits me. And I'm alone.

Where am I?

I look around the room and immediately appreciate the generous space and matching gray tones of the walls and furniture. I smile when I see the life-sized framed artwork of a woman smiling over her shoulder. Though the furnishing is nice and tasteful, the room is somewhat sparsely furnished.

"It's a man's room," I think, and then memories of last night start to filter in.

The feeling of pleasure as he had kissed me returns to a lesser degree. I slide my right palm over my throat, trailing where his lips had kissed. A flame flickers between my thighs, and I can't believe I feel aroused all over again. When I remember the rush when I came, I blush and run a hand through my hair and over my face.

"Well, I know what I need now," I say to myself, common sense returning to my muddled brain. I need to get out of here.

I get up from the bed, picking up my bra from the edge of it and putting it on. I pick up my pants from the floor, wriggling in just as Dayton enters the room. I pause in the middle of getting dressed to study him. In his right hand is a cup with steaming contents; coffee, my nose informs me. He is wearing a white shirt, tucked into his trousers. Even after a night of getting my hands all over his broad chest, I feel my throat go dry as I stare at it again.

"You going to share that?" I ask, tipping my head toward his cup of coffee. I wiggle into my pants all the way, looking around the room for my shirt.

"Sure thing," he says, with a lazy drawl in his tone. He walks toward me, a satisfied glint in his eyes as he hands me the cup of hot coffee.

Normally, I would say something snarky to wipe away that look, but he's currently offering me hot coffee that smells heavenly. And I'm feeling pretty satisfied myself, so I'm sure that look is in my eyes too. I just let it go and accept the cup.

"Thanks," I murmur.

My eyes remain on his as I take my first sip of the coffee. And then they close as the delicious taste of it coats my tongue. *This is another form of ecstasy*, I think to myself. The taste of good, hot, strong coffee in the morning.

"I have a proposition for you," he says.

My eyes flitter open again. His gaze is steady on my face as he looks at me.

"What proposition?" I ask, curious.

His gaze remains steady, but there is now a detachment in his tone as he speaks.

"As a PR effort toward humanizing my image, my team has advised me to get into a relationship. Publicly, that is. Now, while I don't particularly have time for a relationship right now, I realize it doesn't have to be real to be seen as real and gobbled up by the media."

He pauses.

"Now, of course, you would be perfectly compensated for it, should you agree to it. In fact, you can name your price."

He stops and keeps his stare fixed on me as he awaits my response. I blink, finding out that's all I'm capable of doing for the first few seconds.

"It's an odd proposition, I realize that, but seeing as you were the one that walked in on me while I was thinking about it on the roof in the first place...," his voice trails, his lips curling into a wry smile.

I realize the oddity of what's happening right now. I'm standing, half-naked—as I still haven't seen my damn shirt—in the room of a man I know next to nothing about, after a one-night stand with same man. And that man is proposing that I be his girlfriend, fake or not, for financial compensation. It's odd, yeah, but it sure beats waking up in my own bed, feeling miserable about Carl and his new model girlfriend.

I take another sip of coffee and walk over to the small table in the corner of the room. I place the half-empty cup on the table, and my eyes land on my shirt, peeking out from underneath it. I pick it up and put it on. As I start to button it up, I turn to him and tilt my head to the side.

"Why me?"

His eyebrows tilt up in surprise at my question. And then he shrugs.

"Like I said—"

"Yeah, yeah, I stumbled on your alone time on the roof when you were thinking about it. That's it?"

I cross my hands over my chest as I look at him.

"I don't know you all that well, but I get the feeling you're a guy who is very particular about the people he lets into his space. And if I do this, I'll be in your space, a lot. So, why me?" I ask again.

He looks at me for another second, and then he walks over to a corner of the room. His closet, I see as he opens the wooden panel, revealing rows of shirts and suits of mostly black and gray variety. He picks a black suit and turns to me as he puts it on.

"Like you, I don't do this very often," he pauses. Something passes in his eyes, and then he adds, "Never," flatly. The suit slips on him so smoothly like it's made for his body. "And it wasn't as...disappointing, as I thought it would be. With you."

Something clutches at my heart. The words weren't romantic in any way at all, and yet I feel like I've received high praise, especially given they're from a man like Dayton. And even as I think about it, I realize I could do it. But....

"I can't," I say.

Something flickers in his eyes, but he doesn't say anything.

"I am just getting out of a relationship. And while I realize this is going to be a totally surface-only arrangement, I still don't feel it's a good idea for me to jump into another relationship so fast. There is no love lost between Carl and I, believe me. I just don't think it's a good idea."

He nods and turns back to his closet. He selects a shirt and walks toward me. He hands it to me.

"You can think on it," he says.

I look down at the shirt in my hand, and recognizing it as a woman's shirt, my curiosity is piqued. Hadn't he just said he didn't do this very often? My eyes go up to the drawing on the wall, of the woman laughing over her shoulder.

"There's nothing to think about," I say.

He turns to me.

"I'd say there's a lot to think about. Come on, I'll take you to work," he says.

The indignation that had risen up at his first statement dies as the implication of his second statement hits me. My eyes goes wide as I look up at the wall clock.

"Shit! I'm late for work!" I exclaim. "Where the hell are my shoes?"

I look around the room, a thin ball of panic starting to form in my throat. I bend down to look under the bed.

"Here they are," Dayton says.

My head jerks up and I see him holding my shoes by the tips of his fingers.

"You might want to change into a new shirt," he says, indicating the shirt he gave me earlier, which I had thrown on the bed as I searched for my shoes. "You don't want to show up in exactly what you left in yesterday. Tongues might wag."

My eyes narrow as I take my shoes from him. He turns toward the door.

"There's an extra toothbrush in the bathroom," he calls out as he leaves the room.

CHAPTER SIX

Dayton

I study the man in front of me. Lex Cardington. The owner and founder of REFUGE, a relief center for people dealing with depression. Well, it started out as a relief center, but then it morphed into something bigger.

The 65-year-old man with a few gray hairs at his temples stares right back at me. His glare is so intense, it almost makes me squirm in my chair. Dignity and self-preservation keep me still. I also want to break off this eye contact we have going on, but what started out as a harmless study of each another now seems like some sort of test. So, I hold on.

"Do you know what REFUGE is about, Dayton?" he asks, still staring at me in that intense manner.

I relax a bit, because this question, I know the answer to.

"I do. It's a community. Sure, it started out as a refuge, but it became more. It became a place to not only feel safe in, but to also remain safe in. To make a difference in, to build a home in, to become stronger in."

Lex's face remains impassive as I talk. After a few seconds, he nods. He shifts in his chair.

"When I started REFUGE, it was just a small first aid center for depressed people who had gone too far. It was a special kind of hospital for them alone, to be treated by people who knew what they were going through, or had experience dealing with them." He spread out his hands. "With me, I had just two licensed nurses. We were under a canopy for the first six months, with just a privacy screen protecting our patients from probing eyes."

"And now," I pick up from where he left off, "it is a medically licensed standard hospital, focused on depressed patients but also fully equipped for minor injuries, and a central park that is, to me, the most therapeutic place in the small community. A small community comprising of three state-of-the-art relief centers, with licensed and experienced psychologists."

He nods.

"It is. But before it came to be that, it had to go through a lot of adjustments—"

"Yes, a makeshift classroom was constructed in the same building as the relief center," I cut in.

Lex's eyebrows tilt upward in surprise.

I continue.

"It was built for the people who had started to show considerable signs of well-being. They were taught basics on educational subjects. Depending on where they were at in their various schools, before the depression became overpowering. You were the teacher at the time of its creation."

Lex nods slowly.

"Impressive," he says, his eyes steady on mine.

"I like to be embodied with knowledge; it's my way of being prepared," I say.

He tilts his head slightly, regarding me quietly.

"And this preparation, was it done only because you wanted to acquire REFUGE, or because you want to know about REFUGE?" he asks.

"Both," I say without hesitation.

Lex nods again.

"And then," I continue, "even that makeshift classroom morphed into something bigger. A standard college with a very wide range of courses and a college hostel."

I have done enough business deals to know when one is successful. And this one? It is practically in my lap.

I make my closing statement. "I know what REFUGE means, Lex. I know what it started out as, and I know it is way more than that now. REFUGE started basically as that, a refuge."

I pause, my gaze steady on Lex. "Now, REFUGE is a home, and it is a home that many people need. And that is what I intend to continue to make of it."

"You going to change its name, son? If you get it," he adds.

"Something like that," I say.

Lex's eyebrows jump.

"*An Didean,*" I say. "It's Irish, for Refuge."

Lex doesn't say anything for a while; he simply sits and stares.

"It mean something to you?" he asks.

I knew this was coming. So, I clear the ball of pain that had lodged in my throat at his question. I nod.

"Yeah, it does. It does for the person I wished had gone to a place like REFUGE. Before it was too late."

The memories threaten to swarm me, and I push them away. I look at Lex.

"She was Irish."

He says nothing for a while, and then he stands up.

"I have to consult with my people, my lawyers." He pauses, "But unofficially, you have REFUGE. Your price is impressive, and you sealed the whole thing just now."

We shake hands.

He leaves, and I sit back down on my chair. I rub a hand over my chest, where a dull throbbing pain is starting to kick.

Melissa. God, even her name hurts. My eyes go to her framed picture on my desk. Normally, I don't let myself think about her; I've trained myself on the art of it. But, with talk about REFUGE, and what it means, thoughts of her are harder to resist.

I look at the picture; her face smiles back at me. She was always smiling, or at least that is the only way I seem to remember her. That prefect blend of brown and gold flecks in her hair, and her honey-brown eyes that seem to look into my soul whenever she looks at me. Just like she's doing from the picture right now. I close my eyes as a sharp pain squeezes my heart. And out of nowhere, eyes black as night interrupt my thoughts. Iris's eyes. I open my eyes slowly.

Iris.

There is no way to even compare the two women. They are as different as night is from day. Both physically and in personality. Where Melissa had been sweet, almost shy, Iris curses her ex-boyfriend under the rain, at the top of her lungs, on the roof of a building she's never been in before. It had been surprising, and honestly, somewhat irking, when she rejected my proposal of a mutually-benefitting arrangement this morning. I am not used to not getting what I want. I rarely lose a business deal, and on the rare occasions that I do, I just didn't try hard enough. Because I probably didn't even want the deal in the first place. So, yeah, it irks.

I pick up my phone from my table. My first rule of business—know your quarry.

***

I walk into *A ghrá*. The pub is packed, as usual, more patrons than newcomers. The noise level is high, as expected from a fully-packed pub with a live band. My eyes rise to the T.V. screen just above the bar, and I see a picture of my face placed side-by-side with Lex's, with the news of me acquiring REFUGE currently being broadcast. I look down, and I meet Brian's eyes as he stands behind the bar. I walk to one of the stools by the counter, taking my seat.

"You did it," he says. Emotions swirl in his eyes, and I feel a prick of them behind my eyes too.

"I did it," I reply to him.

He nods.

"She'd be proud," he says.

And at that, my chest squeezes painfully with emotion. I nod, and Brian places a Manhattan in front of me. He holds up a glass of his own, and we toast silently. Just as I take a sip of my drink, Brian tilts his head toward the other end of the bar. I place my glass on the counter and look over, and I see Iris seated on a stool, nursing her drink. I look back at Brian; he just smiles and walks away. I stay seated on my stool another second before standing up and walking over to her.

I wait till she feels my presence behind her. Her head slowly rises, her eyes land on my face. Shock, suspicion, in that order, have her eyes narrowing.

"Are you stalking me?" she asks, emphasis on the *stalking*.

I raise my eyebrows, putting my free hand in my pocket.

"Do I look like a person who stalks?" I counter.

She stares at me for another minute, her eyes still narrowed. She looks around briefly, and then sighs.

"Whatever. I don't really care," she says and takes a sip of her drink.

I take the stool beside her, setting my Manhattan on the counter.

"Really? You don't care if you're being stalked? I'd think you'd be more careful about that seeing as this is New York. A city widely known as home for the crazies—serial killers and the likes."

She shrugs, and her delicate shoulders move beneath her top, another silky material. Does this woman wear anything other than silk materials that are designed to torture a man?

Her full black hair is pulled into a ponytail, leaving her face bare and open. Her profile is just as striking as I expect. I'm tempted to stare, to study it, but I quickly look away. I trace her gaze into her drink and wonder what she's thinking that's making her look so lost.

"Yeah, well, I don't think you're going to murder me, because..."

She raises her head as she talks, and she trails off as she looks into my eyes. I feel a electric zing run through my head, leaving me feeling light with a buzz. I feel drunk, and I've barely sipped any alcohol. But maybe I am. On her. I watch those black eyes now as they cloud over, as she no doubt relives yesterday night too. I definitely want more than a taste of her.

Sounds and movement of people still continue on, and I can still hear them, but they come from a faraway place as the buzz between us rings even louder. She looks away, breaking the contact.

"Because what?" I ask, referring to her unfinished statement.

She shakes her head slightly. "Look, um—"

I cut her off.

"You work for ENAMOURED."

She looks at me again, that narrowing gaze coming back.

"Not really selling yourself on the non-stalking there, are you?" she asks.

It's my turn to shrug.

"I don't need to sell myself on anything, because I am not stalking you. I did research you though," I add.

I watch those sexy eyebrows lift again. I wonder why every movement of hers seem to fascinate me.

"You *researched* me?" she asks.

I take a sip from my drink.

"I did. Like you said, I'm a man who likes to know enough about the people around him. We've met, counting tonight, thrice now. We've had sex. And I've proposed a business deal to you. I'd say you are more than just around me."

I pause. She still has the incredulous look on her face, but I think I detect a speculative glint in her eyes.

"And, it's not just me apparently. You're also around a close friend of mine, someone I consider family, actually."

When she just looks blankly at me, I gesture toward Brian at the end of the bar, with my head.

Surprise flickers across her face. "Brian?"

"Two out of the three times we've met has been in here. *A ghrá* a favorite of yours?"

She shrugs.

"Along with like a thousand other people. Look, the bar's great, great drinks, really good customer service. And always so lively with that band that he's got playing every night. And there are always more than enough people in here that you and your problems are able to disappear fairly in the noise. Plus," she shrugs again, "he's a really good listener."

Can't argue with any of the things she just listed. I decide to change the topic.

"Carl Lingstrom is your ex."

I watch her closely, and God, is it a delight? Her eyes flash, that familiar temper sparking.

"How did you—"

I interrupt her again.

"I want to propose our arrangement again," I say.

CHAPTER SEVEN

Iris

"What?!"

I realize my voice comes out sounding like a croak, but I really can't care less.

Who the hell is this man?

"I am reiterating the aforementioned proposal that I made to you this morning," he says. And he says it in that prim businessman tone, like he's talking about acquiring some business deal.

I shake my head a little, trying to sort through the mess in my head.

First of all, "How the hell do you know who my ex is?"

"A number of ways. First, you said his name up on the roof that night. And second, when I researched you."

He looks at me, the cool businessman with steady eyes and an almost bored gaze as he tells me, for the second time tonight, that he had researched me.

"Where the hell do you get off *researching* me? I didn't ask to be in, or around, your life, as you so graciously put it. And I definitely have no desire to continue to be part of your life. So, back off, dude."

To my surprise, amusement glitters in his eyes.

"This is why I am even proposing this a second time. You make things a little less annoying, as I'm absolutely sure you would make this whole annoying affair of getting a public girlfriend, a little less so." He picks up his drink, giving me a little salute with it. "And you're definitely not boring."

A thin thread of warm pleasure tries to work its way through my annoyance. But my annoyance wins. I turn on my stool so I'm facing him directly.

His full and rich black hair sits as prettily as it had done on his head this morning. Like a whole stressful day hadn't gone by for him as it had done for me. Well, seeing as he's a boss, his day was probably not as stressful as mine.

And he definitely looks like a boss, with his primly tailored bespoke suit which highlights his undeniably sexy gym body. Even his pants are doing a grand PR job on his muscled thighs. The button at the neck of his white shirt is loose, revealing a clean slice of his buff chest.

But while the clothing was impressive, the most arresting part of him is his eyes. It had been that first night on the roof, and it was yesterday night as he ravaged me. And it definitely is right now as they stare into me, like they can see through to my soul. And that satisfied, leaning into cocky, definitely smug look? Yeah, Dayton has the sexy boss look on lock.

But, again, I couldn't care less.

"Look, pal, you do not have the right to *research* me, okay?"

He looks like he is about to interrupt me, again. I hold up a hand, cutting him off this time. I'll damn well have my say.

"A lot of people have met three times, more than, and have re-
mained strangers. It's freaking New York. And more than the percent-
age of people who have met each other three or more times are people
who have had one-night stands, like you and I did last night. They
don't go around researching one other, because, one, it's unnecessary,
and two, it's honestly creepy. And if they did, I'm sure they would
definitely not rub it the faces of whomever they researched. It's not
charming, it's not mysterious. It's honestly just creepy and fucked up.
So, stop."

I finish on a whoosh of breath, to find that amused look on his face
again.

"Understood," he says.

I know I should probably press for more, like an apology. But if I'm
being honest with myself, I am more envious that I hadn't thought to
research *him*, more than I'm pissed that he did. So.

And besides, who am I kidding? I look at him out of the side of my
eye, as I turn on my stool, now back to sitting side-by-side with him.
He would never apologize. And that's the honest-to-God fucking fact.

"The research is done, so I'm not going to apologize for it." *See?*
"But I did learn something from it."

He looks at me out of his side-eye. "Your ex has been dating his new
girlfriend for a week. We met a week ago, on the roof."

I stare at him a minute, before tearing my gaze away. I swallow hard,
my Manhattan drink suddenly going sour in my mouth.

Yeah, Carl has been dating fucking Nissa Jenner for a week. Finding
out about it yesterday had been part of the low point of an already
shitty day. And finding out the model Nissa Jenner was part of EN-
AMOURED models today had been the piss on the shit.

Somehow, I know he knows about that little tidbit too. I look at
him out of the corner of my eye again. But he isn't pointing it out.

Well, score for the arrogant alpha-boss.

I sigh, somewhat inwardly, suddenly tired. "Yeah. Just found out about it too."

He doesn't say anything for a bit. "And that's why I'm proposing the arrangement again. You can now have a stake in it too. You, dating me, a top-name, barely a week after the breakup, it's guaranteed to rub some insult in his face."

I chuckle lightly. *Definitely arrogant*, I think to myself. But then, I start to think some more.

I look at him, like, really look at him. And I can see it. Me, on the impressive arm of *him*, cameras flashing, press buzzing. And Carl, oh yes, Carl. Fury is an understatement for what will be on his face when he hears about it.

Oh, I can see it clearly. Just like I can see the sex. The hot, steamy, sweaty sex. Flashes of Dayton over me, as he slides inside me, his broad muscles flexing as they move with the rhythm of his strokes. The sweat glistening on his chest as he grunts with effort, fucking me to oblivion.

"Sex is out," I say abruptly.

"What?" His eyebrows furrow into confusion.

I take deep breaths to still my wildly racing heart and even out my slightly flushed face. I backtrack a bit. "I mean, if we're going to do this, sex is out. We're not going to be having sex," I clarify.

He looks incredulous as he stares at me. "How the hell are we supposed to convince the public, the bloody media, that we're dating, if we're not going to have sex?"

Even though my heart has started to pound wildly again, I merely raise an eyebrow. "People don't wear sex on their faces, Dayton. We're not animals," I say.

Dayton looks at me for another frustrated second.

"Well, sh—"

He runs a hand through his thick hair. I understand his reaction, partly, trust me. Now that I know how cataclysmic sex is with him, I'm kicking myself for suggesting we put it out of the equation. Believe me.

But, it is also the knowing that is making me take it off the table.

I don't know yet if I could fall in love with Dayton. I look over at him. There are shadows in his eyes, secrets that I'm not sure I will ever be able to get to. Or even want to get to. He hides them fairly well actually, but they're there.

And maybe it has something to do with the picture of the woman on the wall that I had seen this morning. And maybe it had nothing to do with it at all. Either way, it has something to do with something or someone. And emotional baggage like that? It pulls me in. If we delve into this arrangement of ours, and add sex to the mix of that, I know I'll get to know him well enough to want to be pulled in.

And just like I am not to him, despite his false claims, he is also not annoying to me. Definitely not boring either. So, yeah, I don't know if I could fall in love with him, but I know I can really come to care. So, I smile at him.

"You'll be fine, researcher. How do we do this?" I ask.

He looks at me a long minute, like he wants to convince me to change my mind on the sex. But then, he lets it go.

Another score for the arrogant alpha-boss.

"My PR team will actually be in charge of that. They'll let us know what we need to, down to the cloths we'll wear."

"Wow, fancy," I say.

He shrugs, a man clearly used to a PR team taking care of stuff for him. "Yeah, well. We can negotiate the price between us though."

I shake my head. "No price. We both have stakes in this. That's enough for me."

He looks at me for a minute, his face not showing any of his feelings. And then he nods. He raises a hand and orders another round of Manhattans for us.

CHAPTER EIGHT

Dayton

I lean against my car, idly turning the car keys in my hand. I'm waiting for Brian to come out of his apartment building.

New York bustles, as it always does, with droves of people walking past, each person absorbed in his certainly chaotic life and completely oblivious to the other person's problems. Cars, cabs, a redhead kid on a bike, whiz past. The crisp morning air hardly chills, doing nothing but reminding me of the possible need for warmer clothes.

I glance over as Brian walks out of the building. His choice of clothing is casual, a blue checkered shirt buttoned half way over a white tee and black jeans.

"Sure that makeup is enough for ya?" I quip, taunting him for taking his sweet time getting ready.

"Bite me, jerkwad," he returns.

I toss the keys at him.

"You're driving. I have some work to do," I say.

Brian just shrugs and walks over to the driver's side. I get in the other side. We both settle in, fastening our seat belts. Brian pulls out into the street.

While Brian navigates the light traffic toward Murray Street, I get busy replying to emails and signing e-documents on my cellphone.

"So, Tessa called me," Brian suddenly says.

My fingers falter a bit over my phone's screen as I experience some surprise over his announcement. Not raising my head up from my phone, I continue typing.

"Oh? What did she want?" I ask.

"She just wanted to check up on you, how you're doing," Brian answers.

"Hmm," I say noncommittally.

Brian lets the silence marinate for five seconds.

"Come on, man, you know she just wants to be in your life," he says.

"She is in my life," I say, just as I send my approval for the plans of a building I acquired two days ago to my architect.

"You know what I mean," Brian says.

I sign off on a document my secretary sent to my email. "No, I actually do not," I counter.

Brian sighs. "They just want to be in your life. I mean, is that so bad?"

When I don't say anything, he adds, "They were not there before, and now they want to be. They're really trying their best, Dayton, and I think you should cut them some slack. They're your parents."

I stop typing as the slow burn that always accompanies talk about my parents steadily rises.

Brian glances at me, I glance back.

"'They were not there before.' That's the key phrase, isn't it? They were not there before, and now they want to be. And just because they want to be, I have to accommodate them now. They couldn't care less when they didn't see me then, and it worked out well for them, didn't it? Why don't we just keep that energy?"

Brian looks like he's about to say something more, so I cut him off.

"I don't want to talk about it," I say, making sure my tone is definite.

I know if Brian wants to really get into it with me, he will. And he's one of the few people in my life I'd let. But, he doesn't.

We continue driving in silence.

Thirty something minutes later, we get to our destination. Seagate, Coney Island.

Brian eases the car to a stop in front of a Victorian-style house with faded gray paint and a porch lined with several pots of brightly colored flowers. We both get out of the car, and even as I look out at the house, Patrick Campbell walks down the short steps of the porch.

Patrick Campbell, a 65-year-old man with a weathered face and few gray strands in his rich black hair, smiles a little as he walks toward us. He stands at just a few inches shorter than me, and his clear gray eyes regard us steadily as we stand side-by-side.

"Boys," he says. His voice is deeply rich, the Irish lilting brogue adding a near musical texture to his speech.

"Hey, Dad," Brian says, hugging him.

Patrick pats him on his back as they separate. He turns to me.

I lean forward to give him a hug of my own. He pats me on my back too as he did Brian.

"You look good," I comment as we separate.

And he really does, I think to myself, as I take in his relaxed countenance.

His eyes crinkle a bit at the corners as he smiles.

"What man wouldn't? Sand, sea, peace and quiet. And of course, man's best friend," he adds, glancing over as his dog, Mill, comes bouncing over to greet us. Mill jumps on Brian's legs, wagging its tail wildly.

Brian laughs and bends down to ruffle him behind the head.

"Any more relaxed, I'll be dead," Patrick finishes.

We both look down at Brian and Mill as Brian continues to ruffle him. And then Patrick shifts his gaze to me. I turn my head as I feel his eyes on me. In the gray of them, I see bone-deep sadness, an understanding that only comes with knowing that sadness, and something else. The something else that always means Patrick sees through me, inside me.

His eyes steady on mine, he addresses Brian. "We're going to take a walk."

Brian looks between the two of us and just nods as he continues playing with Mill.

Patrick starts to walk away from the house, toward the beachfront. I fall into step beside him. I put my hands in the pockets of my pants.

"She'd be really proud of you," Patrick says after we had walked a few steps away from the house.

I feel a dull pain in my chest, and my hands ball into fists in my pockets.

"REFUGE. A solid name with a solid meaning. A very important one too."

Now, Patrick stops and turns to look at me. "I'm proud of you son," he says.

And I feel my throat close up. I stare into his eyes, clear as the water that is currently washing up shore just a few feet away from us, steady on me.

I can't seem to find my voice, to say something back, to appreciate him. But it looks like it doesn't matter as Patrick turns to face the ocean. The breeze ruffles his hair a bit, flapping the ends of his shirt.

"God, she always loved the beach," he says.

And I don't need him to say her name to know we're talking about Melissa. She's the whole reason for this trip. I feel that dull pain in my chest again. I turn to face the ocean too.

I struggle to find my voice, till I do.

"I see Mrs. Mendoza is still bringing over flowers," I say, referring to Patrick's next-door neighbor, and Melissa's friend when she was alive.

Mrs. Mendoza, a 68-year-old Spanish woman with a heart of gold, who had been there all through the while Melissa struggled with depression. Up till the end.

The corners of Patrick's lips tip upward. "Yeah. Lilacs were her favorite, and Artie makes sure they're never in short supply. It feels good to remember her that way. Even though it was sad and painful at the end, it had been bright and cheerful till that point. And it's good to remember that."

I take a moment, trying to find the right words.

"REFUGE is for Melissa. For her and other people like her, who are still alive, who think they have nowhere to go, and no one who understands them. For them to see that they do. That they don't have to drown in the depression." I look out at the ocean as the waves crash right over themselves. "But it's also for you."

Patrick looks at me, and I don't have to look at him to know those gray eyes are steady on me.

"Before I fell in love with Melissa, you helped me fall in love with the three of you. You, Brian, and Melissa. Being there, waiting for me, every day after school. Teaching me how to ride a bike. Teaching me how to fish. Listening to me when I had something to say. Being the father that I needed. You helped me fall in love with the three of you. Because, those moments in the kitchen back at the house in New York, with me, you, Brian, and Melissa, while my parents were off at one charity event or the other, those moments were the happiest of my life. And you did that." I scoff lightly. "Gardener. You were definitely more than a gardener to me. You were my whole world."

I take a breath, and then I turn to look at Patrick, steady right on back.

"So REFUGE is also for you," I say.

The waves splash on the sand inches from our feet, but we don't stop staring at each other. A sheen of moisture dampens Patrick's eyes; he doesn't try to blink it away. He just stares right back at me, all of his emotions unashamedly emblazoned across his face.

And then he pats my arm and turns back to face the ocean. I face the ocean too. And we stare at her waves in silence for a girl we had both loved, in our own ways. And who had loved the ocean.

***

An hour later, I lean my head back on the lounge chair as I close my eyes in bliss.

"Mrs. M hasn't lost her touch," Brian says from his spot on his lounge chair beside me.

The look of total satisfaction on his face mirrors mine.

"Her peach cobbler has always been undefeated, but that blueberry pie may just be the death of me," I say.

"Oh, I'll die a happy man," Brian says.

I smile, my eyes still closed. I open one eye. "Where's your dad?" I ask.

After remembering Melissa by the beach, we went into the house. Mrs. Mendoza must have heard us drive up because we came in to meet her in the kitchen. By then, Brian was starting on the pie she made for him. After the early lunch cum late breakfast, or rather, brunch, Patrick excused himself.

"He says he has some calls to return. He'll soon join us," Brian says.

"Hmm," I mutter.

We're on the terrace beside the house, the waves from the beach whooshing and splashing in the background. And I second Patrick's words from earlier. If I were any looser, I'd be dead.

"So, I saw you and Iris leaving the other day," Brian says.

And I feel my guts coil tightly. There goes my relaxed mood.

I glance over at Brian. "So?" I ask, as casually as I can manage.

"So. You never take women home," he says.

I smirk. "Just because I don't tell you about the women I take to my bed doesn't mean I don't take them. We're not 12-year-old girls."

"I meant you took her to her own home," Brian says. I look over at him, and his eyes—gray like his father's—widen ever so slightly as he stares at me. "You slept with her, didn't you?" he asks.

I mentally curse myself for falling into this one. And then I shrug. Light is how I'm playing it, because there's nothing to be heavy about.

Brian's eyes narrow. "Seriously, dude, what's the deal?"

I raise my eyebrows, a bit surprised at Brian's nosiness. "What's it to you?" I ask.

"She's a friend, Dayton, a really good friend," he says, his tone serious.

I know Brian doesn't say stuff like that carelessly. One point for Iris Siobhan.

"Relax. It's not what you're thinking. We have an arrangement," I say.

Now it's Brian's eyebrows that jump up. "An arrangement? What the hell does that mean?"

"It means exactly that. Now, if you want more info on the topic, you can ask her yourself. You are really good friends, after all."

And I'm looking forward to being more.

Chapter Nine

Iris

IRIS

"**O**kay, this is not at all what I was expecting," I say as my eyes take in my surroundings.

My arm is hooked through Dayton's, and we're walking into a restaurant. Or is it a cozy lounge? It's our first official outing as a couple, though the news of us dating has been leaked to the media a week ago.

The news circulated many of the popular New York gossip tabloids over the week. I had thought my life was crazy before, but this week was eye opening. My life before meeting Dayton Pade was remarkably serene. And now that I've experienced media interest, I can't stop wondering how Dayton lives with all the scrutiny. My life had been dissected into tiny fragments, and I'm not even that interesting.

"Oh? And what had you been expecting?" Dayton asks me.

I look around again, at the sea of people already gathered. The mood is casual, and the outfits generally reflect this, although a good number of women have on outfits that would be better described as inviting, flamboyant, or flat-out racy. The room is abuzz with mild chatter, soft laughing, and the clinks of champagne flutes and cutlery.

White lace table runners cover the tables, and candlelight flickers from within small vases placed on the tables. Music wafts softly through the speakers placed at hidden spots all around the hall.

I scoff lightly. "Just not this," I say, using my hands to indicate the whole room. When Dayton just looks at me steadily, I huff.

"Fine. I guess I was expecting one of those fancy, you know, classy waltzy parties."

I watch as his lips lift up at the sides slightly. My eyes narrow.

"Are you laughing at me?"

Dayton snags two flutes of champagne from the tray of one of the servers as he passes by. He hands one to me.

"Avoiding the question with champagne? I never took you for a coward, Mr. Pade," I say, even as I take a sip of champagne. The flavor is sharp and incisive, simmering on my tongue and leaving instant satisfaction. My eyes are on him, so I see as he smiles slowly around the glass of champagne at his lips.

My heart stutters a bit, and I feel a rush of heat go through my body as the candlelight bounces off his eyes. My gaze involuntarily lands on his lips. His very sinful, and very kissable, lips. He licks a sheen of champagne off his lips, and I feel that heat between my legs intensify. Someone knocks something against some other thing, and I am jarred out of my stupor. I blink, disoriented a little.

I look up at Dayton to see if he had done that on purpose. He hadn't, I realize, as he glances round the room casually. I swallow, willing my wayward heart to be still. I had taken sex off the table; I had been the one to suggest it. Me. So, thinking about Dayton that way will certainly not do. I take a deep breath and paste a smile on my face.

"So, whose company party is this?" I ask.

Dayton's gaze comes back to mine.

"Mine," he says.

My eyebrows jack up in surprise.

"Yours? Well, then why are you not..." I trail off, trying to find the right word. "...hosting?" I finish.

He shrugs lightly, his broad shoulder moving impressively beneath his suit. "I did not throw the party. The company, ECOFOOD, a branch of food company I own, did. And their CEO, Jack Grimes, is, automatically, the host."

"So, you go to parties thrown by every company you own then?"

"No, not really. I came because I actually like this company's CEO. Jack is a friend. And I know the owners of this venue. They're also friends of mine," Dayton says.

I chuckle. "You said you actually like *this* company's CEO. You mean you don't like all of your CEOs?" I ask.

Dayton shrugs again. "Not really. Some of them are assholes. What I require though, when it comes to a CEO of a company I own, first and foremost, is brilliance. Accountability, and a person who knows what the hell he, or she, is doing. And knows it damn well." He lifts his shoulders. "Some of them don't have a great personality to go with it, and that's fine."

I scoff lightly and take a sip of my drink.

"Hey. So I saw you on the news yesterday."

Dayton takes a sip of his drink too. "I'm mostly always on the news," he says.

I smile.

"I know, but I hardly ever watch the news, so, I really didn't know who you were until I screamed on your roof," I say.

Dayton's lips turn up at the sides.

"Okay, so, I saw you on the news yesterday, and what they were talking about was actually some old news. You bought REFUGE."

Dayton nods. "I did."

"Wow. I have always admired the story of that place, and the work the people there do. When I heard Lex Cardington was going to be selling it off, I had hoped it wouldn't be to someone who didn't see its value."

I pause, peering up at Dayton. "You see its value, right?"

I realize it is not my place to ask such a question, but I figure all he has to do is *not* answer if he doesn't want to.

Dayton looks down at me, the candlelight playing over his features.

"I do," he says.

There goes that stutter again.

I smile at him. "Good."

Just then, my gaze lands on the taxidermy on the upper part of wall right above Dayton's head. A deer head taxidermy.

I tilt my head as I study it.

"Huh," I say.

Dayton turns to look at it too.

"What do you think of it?" he asks.

"Well, it's not art, is it? I mean, it's a dead animal. Why hang a dead animal on your wall? On the wall of an event place you rent out to hundreds of people, no less. And now, we have to come here and stare at the dried-up carcass of dead animals. Why would you do that? Why would anyone do that?" I state, sipping from my champagne.

When Dayton doesn't say anything, I turn to look at him, and I find him staring at me, a befuddled look on his face.

"What?"

Just then, a couple walk up to us. The woman is a willowy brunette with skin the color of melted white chocolate and a perfect set of white teeth. The man is six feet tall, maybe inches more, has an eerily similar set of teeth to the woman, and carries a mop of black hair.

"Dayton!" the woman exclaims softly. Her eyes light up with pleasure as she hugs Dayton.

They separate, and instinctively—I don't even think she notices—she molds back into the crook of the man's arm.

"Hey, man," the man shakes Dayton's hand.

"Katie, Alex, meet Iris Siobhan. Iris, Katie, Alex," Dayton introduces.

I shake both their hands.

"Nice to meet you," I say, wondering who they are.

"Katie and Alex are the owners of this venue," Dayton says.

Oh. "You have a really beautiful place here," I say.

Katie beams. "Thank you so much. We like hearing nice things about our place," she says, and laughs.

"How come you guys are here? Figured you'd be as far away from here as possible. I know how you like to take the time off when the venue is rented by someone you trust," Dayton says.

Katie and Alex smile identically. "Yeah. But Jack invited us, and we really felt like getting dressed up and going out. So why not come tonight?" Katie says. We all laugh.

And then Dayton looks at me, looks back at the couple.

"Say, Iris and I were just talking about this taxidermy up here," Dayton says, pointing up at the deer head.

Oh God, what is he doing?

I steal a glance at him and smile uneasily.

"Yes. I was just saying how beautiful it is, how—"

"Was that it?" Dayton cuts me off midsentence.

He tilts his head to the side.

"I don't recall that. What I recall is you saying how it's the carcass of dead animal, and asking why would anyone, *anyone,* you insisted, put something like this up for people to stare at. Isn't that right?"

He looks at me, a saccharine sweet smile on his face. And I want to punch the smug expression off his face. I look over at Katie and Alex, and thankfully, they both had amused expressions on their faces.

"Katie, Alex, I heard this was a wedding present. Isn't that right?" Dayton asks, that saccharine sweet tone still dripping.

Katie looks like she's about to burst out laughing. She nods.

"Yes. Yes, it is," she says.

"Oh, wow. Who gave it you? Can you—can you tell us?" Dayton asks.

And even before Katie bursts out laughing, and Alex follows suit. Even before they both say, "You," I already know.

I look up at Dayton, and then at the taxidermy, and then back at Dayton. And I'm sure the look of utter *what the fuck* is on my face.

Dayton just grins.

***

I come out of the restroom, smoothing a hand down the soft material of my knee-length dress. My gaze is drawn toward the entrance of the restaurant, and I glance over to see a small commotion brewing. The security guy at the door seems to be restricting a guy from entering. And the guy is in the middle of a very determined protest.

I start to walk back toward the party, as the commotion is not my problem to deal with. But then the voice of the man being restricted reaches my ears. I know that voice.

I turn back, and when the security guy's broad shoulders block my view of the other man, I walk toward them. I peer around the security guy's shoulders, and my eyes narrow as I confirm my suspicion.

"Carl?"

Carl's gaze shifts from his quarry to mine. Anger at the security guy for not letting him in and annoyance at being interrupted both fade from his eyes as he focuses on me. And then bafflement takes over his whole face completely.

"Iris? What are you doing here?" he asks.

My eyebrows jump at his question.

"Same thing you're doing here, I imagine. Though I guess not exactly the same," I add, looking pointedly between him and the security guy, who continues to look formidable.

"Carl, baby, who is she?"

As the ditzy looking blonde who hangs on Carl's arm like a sparkly purse talks, my gaze shifts to her. It's no longer Nissa the model, I see.

I hadn't even noticed she was there. And it shouldn't have been easy for me to miss her, seeing as she's wearing a dress almost entirely covered in sparkly, glittering specks. There appears to be some dusting of those glitters on her face too. My eyes feel like they're hurting just by my looking at her.

So I shift my gaze back to Carl. Which—as I take in his overly gelled blonde hair and the baffled look still on his face—is not exactly better, I realize.

"Miss Siobhan, do you know these people?"

I turn to the security guy as he asks me this question. He is a tall, burly looking man with an expressionless look on his face. And a twinkle in his eyes.

I smile up at him, and then turn to look directly at Carl.

"No. I do not," I say.

And I don't give two fucks how small it seems. I feel giddy delight when I see the shocked look on Carl's face. His mouth actually opens into a small 'o'.

I smile at him, saccharine sweet. "Close your mouth, honey, you don't want to look like a trout, do you?" I look at the ditzy blonde. "You too, sparky."

I turn and walk back into the party, a wide smile on my face.

CHAPTER TEN

Dayton

DAYTON

I t's been two days since the ECOFOOD company party, and I and Iris's first official outing as a couple. And, while I'm seated in my boardroom with my executives and directors, and while we're in the middle of a very serious meeting about one of my companies' stock market problems, I am also chatting with Iris.

I am nothing if not a multitasker.

"I think FIT IS FIT needs to be sold, it's too much of a risk otherwise," Ross Byron, one of my accountants, says.

Kim Bernardo, one of my lawyers, smirks at him. "Oh, you *think*, do you? Well, I guess since you think then," she shoots back, sarcasm dripping heavy in her tone.

Ross's hand balls into a fist on the table, and I, along with every other person in the room, watch him as he visibly tries to restrain himself. Now, of course, he would never hit her. As he is neither an asshole, nor a jackass. But Kim raises his hackles so.

"This is a company board meeting, Kim," he says through gritted teeth. "I am an accountant. My job is to give my opinions on the financial states of establishments owned by this company. If you don't like my opinions, keep those thoughts to yourself, will you? No one asked you."

Ross's tightly wound countenance doesn't seem to faze Kim in the slightest, as she just tilts her head slightly to the side.

"You are really good at stating the obvious, Ross. Perhaps you should have been a kindergarten teacher. You would have done everyone a favor, because then you would have been doing what you were born to do. You would have been happy, and that stick up your butt wouldn't be there. Or, it wouldn't be so far up, at least. I don't think you can live without the stick."

Kim folds her hands on the table like she's talking serious business. "And me? I would have been spared having to think about what it was exactly that I did wrong in my former life, every time I see your face."

She gives Ross a small hateful smile.

Ross leans on the table, a wide, oval-shaped oak table currently surrounded by three executives, two directors, two lawyers, four accountants, and my secretary. He and Kim are on opposite sides of the table, facing each other directly. An arrangement I suspect they intentionally make every single time.

Ross starts to retort at Kim's comment, but I tune him out. I look down at my phone's screen, willing Iris's message to come through.

The 'typing' dots appear, and after a few seconds, her reply comes in. Her reply to our ongoing conversation about giving taxidermy as a wedding gift. Unique, or weird?

"Giving taxidermies as wedding gifts is not unique, Pade, it's just weird (cross-eyed emoji)"

I smile as I read her text. I type back.

"Oh, and you're the queen of gift giving. Little miss magic cube for her boss's birthday."

Typingdots.

"How did you know that?!"

"Told you I researched you. That included company's social media account."

Typingdots.

"Creepy. And anyway, she, my boss, loved playing with magic cubes when she was young. She told us herself."

"Yeah, she liked playing with them. When she was twelve."

More dots.

"(middle finger emoji)"

A little chuckle bursts out of me. I glance up to see Kim and Ross are still at it. I turn back to my phone.

"So, what are you doing right now?"

Typingdots.

"Sticking needles and pins in my eyes (GIF of Madonna rolling her eyes in boredom)"

I chuckle again.

"Thought you were living the dream??"

Typingdots.

"Yeah, right now, the dream feels like a nightmare. If I'm asked to fetch one more coffee today, I swear to God..."

"You're asked to fetch coffee?"

Typingdots. And then nothing comes through. Typing dots again. Still nothing. Typingdots, again.

"I was going to start rambling to you about my crappy day, and sometimes crappy job, but I'm not gonna do that."

My eyebrows draw together as I type.

"Why?"

'Why?' Why am I asking that? I wonder to myself. And why do I really want to hear the answer.

Typingdots.

"Because we're not real, Dayton, remember?"

My eyebrows draw together again as I read Iris's text. Because I *had* forgotten for a while.

I look at Kim and Ross, both of them now on their feet as they obstinately make their points.

"Be ready. I'm coming to pick you up."

Typingdots.

I stand up from my chair. Eyes turn to look at me. I pick up my suit jacket from the back of my chair and turn to address the room at large.

"Meeting is adjourned, gentlemen, ladies. I'll have you know my final thoughts on the matter," I say.

I walk out on confused looks and baffled expressions.

"But—" Ross's voice cuts off as I close the door behind me on the way out.

As I walk toward the elevators, I glance down at my phone. Iris has replied. I enter the elevator.

"For what?"

The door closes.

***

For the second time this week, I lean against my car and wait for someone. And a few seconds later, Iris walks out of her office building.

She has on a silky cream-colored top with the neckline shaped into a V that reveals quite a bit of cleavage. A bow, tied from the excess material of the top, rests on the top of the V-neck, obscuring my view of her cleavage in annoyingly efficient fashion. And as she walks toward me, her fitted black skirt leaps above her knee, exposing delicious miles of creamy smooth skin. Her hair cascades in waves of black over her shoulders, the morning breeze ruffling the waves. As I take all of her in, a ball of heat hits my gut and lowers into my groin. I clear my throat as if that'll do anything to help.

'*For what?*' she had asked. I hadn't known the answer to it. All the way from my office till I got here, I still hadn't known. She stops in front of me, hands on her hips, hair blowing wildly in the wind, and that fire in her eyes. A slow-burning trail of desire winds through me, going straight down between my legs.

I guess another part of my anatomy had known, I think to myself.

Iris snaps her fingers in front of my face.

"Yo. Why did you come over here?" she asks.

I put my hands into my pockets before I give in to the temptation to tug on the tips of her hair.

"My lawyer and accountant were fighting," I say.

Her eyebrows jump up. "That a normal occurrence for them?"

I shrug. "About two times a week. Sometimes three when Kim is in that time of the month, I think."

Iris's lips twitch. "Oh really? So what do you do then? As the President of the company."

I pretend to think about it. "I don't pay myself enough money to interfere," I say.

Now Iris laughs. And I experience another winding feeling through me at the sound. But this time, it's mild. And it wraps around my heart instead of my balls.

FAKING IT WITH MY ENEMY

She stops laughing, her eyes on me. "What are you doing here, Dayton?" she asks.

"I came to take you to lunch," I say, on the fly.

She blinks, and I watch as she processes the information. She looks at me with bafflement.

"Lunch?" she asks.

"Yeah. I'm not a real boyfriend, and we're not friends," I say.

She looks into my eyes.

"No, we're not friends," she agrees.

"Right. But, I'm hungry, and I bet you are too. So, let's eat," I say, liking the idea the more I talk.

Iris looks at me for another few seconds, and then she shrugs.

"Fine, but I usually just grab a special from Enzo's," she says, gesturing vaguely behind her. I don't have a lengthy break."

"Enzo's would be?" I ask.

"Oh, a food truck, just right around the corner from here," she says.

She starts to walk, and then abruptly stops. She turns to me, an apologetic look on her face.

"Oh, you probably don't eat roadside food trucks," she says.

I give her a look and simply start walking. She moves too, to keep up.

"The only reason why I would feel squeamish about eating Enzo's is because I have my own food truck regular. Right in front of my office building. Serves the meanest tacos," I say, not even bothering to hide my boast.

Iris smiles up at me. "Okay," she says, surprise evident in her voice. "Well, Enzo's tacos will send your little *regular* hiding."

And two minutes later, taking my second bite into it, I am inclined to agree.

Damn, Enzo knows his tacos.

"Hmm. Okay, this is art," I say after swallowing.

Iris smiles widely. We start walking back toward Iris's office building, tacos in hand.

"So, what were your accountant and lawyer fighting about?" Iris suddenly asks.

"Oh, just some business deal," I say, waving it off.

Iris looks at me, and then she nods. "Right. Sorry, I shouldn't have asked," she says.

I'd be deaf not to hear the distance in her voice, and stupid not to know the meaning. I am neither. I wait a beat.

"They were at odds about the fate of one of my companies," I say. "FIT IS FIT. It's a fitness company in California. My accountant seems to think the cost of fixing its myriad damaged parts is more than what the company is actually worth. He's advising me to cut my losses."

"And your lawyer doesn't agree," Iris says after a pause.

"She doesn't. She's mostly just disagreeing to spite Ross. My accountant. But she brings up some important points too."

I wipe my hand with the paper napkin given to me by Enzo. "I would be breaching the contract I drew up with FIT IS FIT, if I back out now."

"And they could sue you?" Iris asks.

"Actually, no, there's a clause in the contract that prevents them from doing that. I cover my bases," I say.

Iris looks at me.

"I bet you do," she says. "Okay, so there's no real loss in breaching the contract then."

"Well, I'd have to pay some certain amount to them. But it's nothing compared to revamping the whole company. It's a mess."

Iris doesn't say anything for a while, as she seems to be thinking about it.

The gentle afternoon breeze wafts over our faces, and people walk past us with varying speed. I realize how nice walking with Iris like this is. I realize I suddenly want to take her hand in mine, so I put my hands in my pockets instead.

"Seems like the answer is clear here," she says, "but there's something stopping you from taking your accountant's advice, and cutting your losses."

She pauses, and looks at me. "What is it?"

I look at her too, and then I shrug.

"I still believe we have the finances to revamp it. And Ross will too, if he wasn't playing it so safe. Anyway," I shrug again, "I don't have any particular attachment to the company that's making me want to keep it, per se. But it, being damaged and all, it just seems to me like it's asking to be taken a chance upon."

I stop talking because I realize I'm being sentimental. With Iris. And about business. Two things I never do.

At that point, we get to Iris's workplace and stop walking.

Iris turns to me, a small smile on her face. She cocks her head. "FIT IS FIT sounds awfully like a human being, doesn't it? I like that. I think you do too," she adds.

She starts walking backward toward the entrance of the ENAMOURED.

"Lunch was nice," I say.

She smiles. "It was."

She turns and walks into the company.

CHAPTER ELEVEN

Iris

I push open the glass doors into ENAMOURED. As I walk across the lobby, I turn to see Dayton get into his car. Smoothly, he maneuvers out of his parking space, back into traffic.

I turn back to continue walking toward my cubicle. I get to my desk and take my seat, thoughts of Dayton and our conversation occupying my head. And then I catch my reflection in the pocket-size mirror on my desk, and my smiling face stares back at me. I automatically smooth the smile out.

Why am I smiling? I mean, nothing is funny. At least not particularly. So why am I smiling?

I shrug away the twitch in my shoulders. The universe whispers the truth in my ears.

Dayton is...interesting, I decide. Yeah, interesting. That's why I find myself smiling, and, apparently, also thinking about him. I hold off for three seconds—okay, two—before I give in and open my laptop on my desk.

I type 'FIT IS FIT California' in the Google search bar. Images and articles flood out. I click on a full image of the building, and a charming brownstone building fills my screen.

"Oh," I whisper to myself, melting as I scroll through more images. "This is beautiful."

And then I click on articles about the company, clients filing complaints and the company's stock market going all the way down as a result. As I scroll through the comments, my eyes get drawn to one.

"I don't know why FIF is being dissed, but I really enjoyed my membership there when I still lived in California. The equipment was great, the service even better. And I met my boo, now husband there. FIF will always have a special place in my heart, just for that."

I smile as I read the comment. After only a momentary hesitation, I take a screenshot of the page. And after another brief hesitation again, I send it to Dayton. With the caption, *"People are looking for their boos, Pade. Don't be a spoilsport by ruining their fun."*

I smile as I send it. He's probably still driving, I decide. My thoughts get interrupted as his reply comes in.

"Oh, well, then, far be it from me to block love."

I smile as I type back.

"Oh yeah, you don't want to be Cupid's other mean brother."

Typingdots.

"No one wants to be that guy."

I laugh as I read his text. I start to text back, and just at the same time, Alyssa bursts into the room.

My eyebrows jack up at the expression of shock on her face. Her fair skin is flushed, and she is breathing heavily as she looks at me.

"Something wrong, Alyssa?" I ask.

She walks over to my desk, on shaky feet it would seem, as she leans heavily on my desk.

"Iri—, oh my God, Iris," she breathes, more than says, the words.

I grip her arm. "Jesus, Alyssa, spit it out. You're freaking me the hell out. What is it?"

"Lisa wants to see you," she says, her eyes on me.

Thinking of Lisa Banks, a senior designer of men's suits, and one of my direct bosses, I stand up from my chair. "Okay, I'll go down there now and—"

My sentence gets cut as Alyssa grips *my* arm now.

"Ow!" I exclaim at the tightness of her hand.

"No, Iris, Big Lisa," she says.

My brain shuts down as I stare at Alyssa's face. Big Lisa. Big Lisa is what we call Lisa Marion, the owner and president of ENAM-OURED. Four-time *Fashionably* award winner, and three-time *Style* winner. Featured in *Vogue* two times, and the New York Times thrice. Overall fashion mogul and my personal idol.

That Lisa wants to see me.

"Big Lisa wants to see me," I whisper, my brain still dead but for that single sentence running around in it.

Now it's Alyssa's turn to be the coherent one. She walks around my desk to stand in front of me. She takes both my hands in hers. She gives me a hard shake.

"Yes. Now, you're going to go up there, and you're going to listen to what she wants to say. You're going to nod when necessary, and you're going to be coherent when you need to be. She's not firing you," Alyssa says.

Even through the fog in my brain, I follow her reasoning. "She's not going to fire me," I repeat Alyssa's words. "She doesn't take on tasks like that," I say.

Alyssa nods. "Exactly. She's too important for that. So whatever she must be calling you for, it's important. Iris."

She shakes me again till I'm looking at her.

"It's important," she says again.

I look into her eyes; I know what she's saying. This is the break I've been working for ever since I joined ENAMOURED. This is the turning point for my career. And the implication of that knowledge is apparently enough to slap life into my dead brain. I nod at Alyssa and squeeze her hand before letting it go. I turn to walk toward the elevator.

Life in my brain or not, my legs are watery and a sick ball of panic lies in the pit of my stomach as I walk out of the elevator seconds later.

I walk toward the receptionist's desk. A perky-looking young woman with a head of red curls looks up at me. Her smile is the perkiest smile I've ever seen. And it does nothing to ease the sickness in my stomach.

"Hi! I'm Lorraine, how may I help you?"

"Um, I'm Iris. Iris Siobhan. Big—Mrs. Marion wants to see me?"

"Oh, yeah, go right in," Ms. Perky says.

"Thanks," I mutter.

I turn toward the glass doors she points at. LISA MARION. 'President' is printed in big bold letters across the door. I knock once before I push open the doors.

I open the doors into a wide airy space. A large desk and Lisa's chair are situated in the middle of the room, with the visitor's chair facing her. The room is surrounded by glass walls, with a gray sofa covering almost the entire left wall. A coffeemaker and a couple of framed family pictures rest on a table not too far away from the desk. The platoon of awards flank the pictures.

And my eyes automatically fix on the woman herself. She stays seated on her chair. Her cool eyes study me as I walk into the office.

"Miss Siobhan," she says, her voice as cool as her eyes, and heavy laden with a Brooklyn-born tang. "Have a seat."

I walk toward the visitor's chair, fighting the urge to squirm because of the intensity of her tracking eyes. I sit and force myself to look at her. I am not a shy person, neither am I timid, but the reputation of Lisa Marion that I had built in my head over the years is as high as a freaking castle.

So, yeah, I'm uneasy.

"Do you know why I called you up here, Miss Siobhan?" Lisa asks.

Probably best not to think of her as Big Lisa while I'm sitting in front of her, I think to myself.

"No, ma'am," I say, my hands clasped in my lap. I force myself to relax my tense muscles.

"You're aware you've become more popular these days, no?"

I blink. "Um—"

"Since you started dating Dayton Pade," she says.

I stare at her, my mind scrambling to process what her statement means.

Lisa's eyes narrow slightly. "You know VIVID is one of our biggest rivals, right?"

I nod my head, because yes, this I do know. "Yes, I know. But what does this..." I trail off as a new sinking feeling settles in my stomach. "Dayton Pade owns VIVID," I say.

Lisa's eyes steady on me, her lips curl slightly.

"You didn't know," she says.

I swallow. "No. No, I didn't."

Lisa nods slowly as she seems to ponder that. "Well. Be that as it may, it doesn't change the reason for bringing you in here."

She pauses and looks directly at me. "You are going to be presenting your designs at the company's next design show in two weeks."

And for the second time today, my brain goes dead.

I stare at Lisa, trying to compute what she just said. And Alyssa's face flitters into my mind as her words run through my mind.

This is important.

I blink. "I am?" I ask, just to be sure.

"You are," Lisa confirms. She steeples her fingers together.

"You will get the chance to showcase your designs in front of myself, senior designers of ENAMOURED, and other senior designers we invite from other companies. Even VIVID," Lisa adds, looking at me steadily.

I gulp, not physically, but mentally.

"Apart from designers, critics will be there too. Well, you know all about it already." She flicks her hand, waving it away.

And finally, the whole thing sinks in, and I comprehend the enormity of what I'm hearing.

"Oh my God," I breathe. I clasp my hand to my chest. I can feel tears coming on, and I try to hold them back because I don't want to blubber all over Lisa's floor.

"Thank you so much," I say to her.

She smiles, slightly. "Don't thank me. Design."

When I nod enthusiastically, she leans forward on her desk.

"There's one more thing. It's my job as the president of ENAMOURED to know my rivals, and to know them well. And I know Dayton Pade."

She pauses, looking right at me.

"He runs a tight ship, and his employees are loyal to him. Very. There would be nothing more effective than having a direct inside person. And nothing I would appreciate more," she adds.

And the muscles I had ordered to relax tighten several times more. A cold feeling passes through me. I look right back at Lisa.

"You want me to spy for you?" I ask, wanting another confirmation.

"You are a smart lady, Miss Siobhan, you know what I'm asking of you," Lisa replies.

I stare at Lisa, and the saying 'Never meet your heroes' runs through my head.

Well, fuck that, I think to myself. How about the heroes be decent fucking human beings.

"I'm sorry, I can't do that," I say.

Lisa's eyebrows draw together, surprise filters across her face. "May I ask why?"

The cold spreads to my heart.

"I don't think there should be a reason for not wanting to be a mole," I say.

Lisa looks at me for a minute, and then she nods. "Fair enough." She doesn't say anything for another minute, and then, "Well, I guess that concludes our business."

I look at her. I am not sure what that means in regards to showing my designs at the design show. But I'll be damned if I'll ask.

I stand up from the chair, and turn to go.

"See you in two weeks," Lisa says behind me.

My steps halt; I turn to look at her.

Lisa's eyebrows jump up. "Problem?" she asks.

I shake my head and turn again to go. I stop after taking a few steps. I turn back to face Lisa.

"Why were you a jerk just now?" I ask.

Lisa's eyebrows jump up again. And this time, along with the surprise on her face, there is a little amusement too.

"Because I'm the boss. I have to be a jerk sometimes," she says.

I think about it.

"Your job sucks," I say matter-of-factly.

The amusement spreads into a smile.

"It does," she concurs.

I turn to go, finally. A smile spreads across my face as I open the door and walk out.

Guess my hero's cool.

And then, as I get to Ms. Perky's desk, my conversation with Lisa comes flooding back.

"Oh damn," I mutter to myself. I grip Perky's desk to steady my suddenly watery legs again.

Ms. Perky looks at me with concern. "Are you okay?" she asks.

I look at her, and a smile spreads wide across my face.

"Oh damn!" I say, with a delicious mixture of fear and excitement.

CHAPTER TWELVE

Dayton

I stare down at my phone as I push open the door to *A ghrá*. Still no response, I notice, as Iris still hadn't replied my message. A message I had sent since early this morning.

And I'm acting like a teenage girl, I realize in disgust.

I push my phone into my pocket, striding to one of the bar stools. Brian comes over with a glass of Manhattan. I look up at him, and I scowl at his raised eyebrows.

"What?" I snap at him.

I take a sip of my drink. A deep gulp, really. I can feel a pissy mood climbing up my back. I hate pissy moods.

Brian wipes down the countertop in front of me. "Stressful day?" he asks.

I shrug, the tension in my shoulder blades remaining tightly coiled.

"Something like that. Some low-level employee at one of my ac-counting firms created a clusterfuck today by entering the wrong data in one of the company's ledgers."

I take another sip of my drink.

"And when I called for her to come to my office, she was shaking like a leaf because she was afraid I was going to fire her. She looked barely old enough to legally buy a drink. Jesus."

I rub a hand over my face, tired to my bones.

Brian cleans a glass cup with a white napkin as he stares at me. "So, what did you do?"

I shrug. "I had to give her a dressing down. Messing up that way? If I didn't, it wouldn't be logical. And it would probably undermine my authority a bit."

Brian scoffs. "You know your authority is as solid as ever."

Annoyance flitters through me. "So, what? You think I wanted to do it?"

"I never said you did," Brian says, his calm tone not wavering. "How did she get home?"

"How did who get home?"

"The employee who caused the clusterfuck," he clarifies.

"What does that matter?" I ask.

"You told your driver to take her home personally, didn't you?" he asks. "And she'll be fine, eventually. You know that. So, what's gotten in your craw?"

I roll my shoulders uncomfortably. "Nothing is in my craw."

I take another sip of my drink.

"I haven't seen Iris in a while," Brian says suddenly. "You talk to her recently?"

I know he's baiting me, but even knowing doesn't help me control my reaction.

"Why are you asking me? I'm not her keeper, am I?"

Shit.

Brian just smiles. "You've got something in your craw, my man. I suggest you go get it out."

Brian gives me a look before walking away to another end of the bar.

I brood into my glass. I take my phone out of my pocket and check. Still no reply.

I take another sip of my drink.

Something in my craw, I scoff at the phrase. It's a stupid phrase, but if it's the one we're doing with, then fine. I guess I'll just have to get the damn thing stuck in my craw out then. When I have a problem, I fix it. I don't brood into my drink.

I stand up from my stool and walk toward the pub's entrance. And walk out into the busy night and street. I get into my car—I still remember Iris's address from the day I took her home when we first met.

Ten minutes later, I pull over in front of her apartment building. And I have somehow managed to work myself up even more in the ten minutes it took to get here. And now I am even more steamed than I was when I left *A ghrá*.

It's just common courtesy to reply to a message, damn it.

I walk into the lobby and stop short as I realize I don't know her apartment number. I take my phone out again and place a call to Karen, my head of PR. She answers on the first ring.

"I need Iris Siobhan's apartment number," I say, cutting straight to the chase.

"Wha—I don—"

"I know you went up to her house when we were still discussing the contract details. You wanted to make her feel more comfortable." I digress enough to feel grateful for Karen.

"Thank you for that, by the way." I pause. "Now the apartment number, Karen."

Karen sighs. "4B."

"Thanks." I end the call.

I walk into the elevator and punch in her floor. Seconds later, the elevator doors slide open to reveal a corridor with doors on either side.

I walk straight over to apartment 4B, and as I lift my hand to knock, I hesitate. And that hesitation pisses me off, so I knock. It's then I realize loud music is pumping in the apartment.

When nobody answers the door, I knock again. Harder. And then, finally, the door opens. And Iris fills the doorway.

And I get my first gulp of fresh air in days. Her wild black hair is packed up in a messy bun on her hand, leaving strands falling all over her face. She is wearing a shirt that says *Thank God I'm female* and is two sizes too small for her. The shirt stops at her navel, leaving the lower part of her stomach bare. And the shorts she's wearing cover just about the area from her waist to where I imagine her ass ends. Leaving the creamy skin of her long legs bare. The view is delicious.

Thank God, indeed.

Her eyebrows furrow, and surprise coats her face as she looks up at me.

"Dayton?" she says, and it comes out breathless, like she had been doing some exercise in there.

Her creamy legs end on her feet, which are bare, and I can see her toenails are painted a bright red. Her breasts heave slightly under her too-small shirt, and her fingernails are painted a reflective blue. Her face is flushed, and that wild tumble of black hair completes the sinful picture that she makes.

The desire slams hard into me, going straight to my groin.

Chapter Thirteen

Iris

IRIS

I stare at Dayton, and a frisson runs through my body, stirring the pool between my legs.

He still has his suit on, and the fitted way in which it sits on him gives him a clean-cut, James Bond kind of look. The suit doesn't even hide the expanse of his broad shoulders, not even a little. His pants hug his long, lean legs.

As I look at his face, I realize he is currently scowling at me. There's something secretly excitable about it. I feel that frisson again. To offset it, I snap.

"What are you doing here?"

Anger flashes across his face. "We're going to do this out in the corridor?"

"Do what?" Even as I'm asking the question, he's already pushing past me into my apartment. I turn to face his back. "Hey! I didn't say you could come in."

He turns to look at me.

"Don't push me, Iris," he says, his voice low and dangerous.

I should probably feel fear right now. His stare is hard and angry, his glare unflinching. His pose is stiff and erect, his frame taut with obvious tension. And that low voice that indicates he's not here to play.

But maybe it's the stress of the past three days, of trying to come up with a design that will impress the senior designers and Lisa at the design show. Maybe it's that, I don't know. I just know that instead of fear, I feel my own hackles rise too.

"Don't you push me, too. You literally just did, but don't, metaphorically," I say. And I'm sure my eyes are now flashing with that spark my friends tell me they see when I'm angry.

There's a flash of heat in Dayton's eyes as he looks at me, and I am transported back to the first night we had sex. I can feel the blood rush into my head as my heart starts beating fast. My room is suddenly too small, and all the air seems to have been slowly sucked out.

Dayton jerks his eyes away from me; he flexes his bunched fist. His jaw locks as he obviously struggles to get himself under control too.

"Will you turn that damn music off?" he asks.

I angle my head up.

"No," I say defiantly.

He grits his teeth. He looks around my room and starts walking, taking in my apartment.

"I texted you, Iris, since this morning. Why didn't you reply?" he suddenly asks.

I glance at the cut-out materials on my design board, and my sewing materials all scattered over my work desk.

I walk over to reduce the volume on the speaker; the damn thing is starting to give me a headache anyway. But I don't turn it off, so rock music still pounds out, but in the background now.

"I've been busy," I say.

Dayton turns around to face me. "Yeah, for like three days now," he says.

Annoyance bubbles inside me at his tone.

"I didn't know I was supposed to be at your beck and call, my lord," I say through my teeth.

Annoyance flickers through Dayton's eyes again.

"Don't use that tone with me," he says.

"I'll do whatever I damn well please," I return.

Dayton looks like he's about to say something, but then he rethinks. He balls his hands into fists again, a method he obviously uses to calm himself down.

"We have an agreement," he finally says, through gritted teeth. "And you being present and around *is* part of that agreement."

Guilt wars inside me, but I'm not letting go of the anger to feel it.

"Yeah? Well, I have a life too, and I'm not neglecting it cause you want to play boyfriend and girlfriend," I say.

"And an explanation for what has kept you so busy all this while is too much?" Dayton asks, his own eyes flashing with annoyance.

My skin hums as his eyes fix on mine, and I feel that breathless rush start up in me again.

"I haven't even come up for air enough to *think!* Sorry if I didn't think to check in with you," I say.

I can feel my cheeks on fire, and I know my face is flushed now. But is it anger or desire that has it that way?

I'm still trying to figure the answer to that when Dayton starts walking toward me. Slowly.

"All I'm asking for here is some goddamn responsibility," he says.

His voice is at that low dangerous volume again, and I gasp as he stops directly in front of me.

And I continue to look into his eyes, because I realize I can't look away. And I feel trapped, arrested. By his gaze, by his whole being.

It's like a predator to its prey.

But I am no one's damn prey.

Dayton's chest heaves slightly as he stares at me. His eyes trail down to my lips. So I run my tongue over my bottom lip, leaving a sheen of wetness. His eyes go hot, and his nostrils flare up slightly.

Got you.

And then we're on each other. Our lips fuse together, and I lift my hands to interlock them around his neck. His hands come around my waist, and he pulls me to his body. His fingers caress my bare midriff, and that frisson runs through my body again.

Hard rock music pounds out of the speakers, in tune with the fervor of our kiss.

Dayton's hard lips cover mine, and my hands find their way into his hair. I want to get closer. I plaster my body even more to his, wanting more contact.

Suddenly Dayton lifts my legs up, and I wind them around his waist. I moan into his mouth as my head pounds loudly. Dayton starts walking, and few seconds later, my back hits the wall. We separate a bit, and because of the position we're in, I look down into his eyes. Eyes dark with desire, his breath spurting out in short pants. It feels like my whole body is burning, and only when we're kissing does the burn ebb a bit. So, I press my lips to his again, at the same time removing his suit jacket. Our lips still fused together, Dayton helps me by shrugging out of it.

"Your shirt. Remove your shirt. Too many clothes," I breathe, clawing at his shirt.

At that moment, I realize I'm still wearing clothes too. I move to pull my top over my head, but Dayton places his hand on mine to stop me.

His eyes focus intensely on my nipples, and I look down to see them jutting through the fabric of my shirt.

"Leave it," Dayton says, his voice rough and coarse.

And my head falls back on the wall as his lips close over one of them. "Ah!"

I don't realize when I moan out loud as Dayton proceeds to drive me crazy with his mouth on my nipple.

His teeth graze over the hard peak, slowly, and then his tongue circles it. He puts the whole peak into his mouth, and a blinding desire slams into me, hazing my vision.

"Dayton," I breathe out his name.

He continues on to my second nipple and gives the same attention to it. And then, finally, he lifts up my shirt, and my breasts tumble out. He stares at them for a second, before burying his face in them again.

My hands yank at his hair, over his bare shoulders, back in his hair, as his lips close over the bare version now. He nips, sucks, flicks, licks.

"Oh God, Dayton," I moan.

And then he lets go. He slides me down, and I hold on to him because my rubbery legs won't hold me up.

"You drive me crazy, baby," he says, looking down at my nipples. He brings his eyes to mine. "Now I'm going to return the favor."

Before I can comprehend, he turns me around, and now I'm facing the wall.

Surprise, and a delicious thrill runs through me. I shiver as Dayton pulls down my shorts. And then, "Ah!" I let out a moan as his fingers close over my sex.

"Oh God, you are so wet, baby," Dayton groans in my ear as his fingers slide over my clit.

I move my hips, wanting to get closer, wanting his fingers to be in me. But he just continues to torment me by sliding them over my wet folds and not inside them.

"You're wet for me, baby, aren't you? Hmm?" he whispers in my ears. And that delicious thrill vibrates through my body as he licks my ears with the tip of his tongue.

"Oh, Dayton. Jesus," I moan as his fingers continue to slide over my clit, and his tongue works its magic in my ear.

And then, when the pleasure in my clit rears up to an impossible height, Dayton's fingers slip between my folds. And I see exploding colors.

His fingers bury deep inside me, and then they start moving.

"I'm going to make you come all over my hand, baby. You're going to scream my name as I drive you crazy with my fingers."

My body starts to shake as Dayton's breath at my ear coupled with his fingers in my sex evoke mad feelings of pleasure in me.

"Oh, God!" I scream as I grip Dayton's hair in my hands from behind me. His fingers pounds into my sex mercilessly, and his second hand comes up to grab my breasts.

"I said say my name," Dayton growls in my ears.

He continues to move his fingers. And even though I can barely see straight from the blinding pleasure, I hear myself say, "Harder."

"Oh, you want it harder. Don't you, baby?" Dayton whispers into my ears.

I'm close to weeping.

"Yes," I say.

"Then take it," Dayton says, introducing yet another finger inside and increasing the pace of his pounding.

My whole body starts to shake, I feel the blinding pleasure build up in me. It pounds beneath my skin with the effort of Dayton's hands, and the hard rock music still coming out of the speaker. I feel the pleasure in my breasts, as Dayton kneads them with his hand, flicking my nipples simultaneously. And then where the pleasure is the most, the base of my stomach. I see blinding white as the pleasure builds here; Dayton's fingers don't relent.

"Scream my name," Dayton growls in my ear.

And the pleasure shoots straight through me.

"Dayton!" I scream, as waves of shock vibrate through my entire body.

My body shakes with the pleasure, and shakes, and shakes, till I'm certain I'm going to die from it.

And then I slowly start to come down from my orgasm. Dayton takes his hand out, and I see it is slick wet. While I'm still breathing hard from it, Dayton turns my head with his other hand to face him. With eyes black with arousal, he locks on to my face.

"My goodness, you're so beautiful," he whispers.

He smacks my sex. Once, twice, and then nonstop. The effect is a shocking turn, a painful, stimulating delight. The tapping sends tremors that shake my deepest parts and trigger yet another avalanche. A violent orgasm crashes through me, and my sex erupts with a geyser of hot streaming water.

"Oh, oh! Oh my God!" I scream, my legs vibrating.

Dayton releases the belt in his trousers, drawing his trousers down.

"My turn," he growls.

He bends my back even lower, takes a full hand of my hair in his grip and pulls my head back so I can see him over my shoulders. His eyes question, and I answer verbally.

"Still on the pill," I say.

"Thank God," he says.

He guides his cock into me slowly and groans against my neck as he buries himself fully inside me.

"Ah, fuck, baby," he says.

"Fuck me, Dayton," I say.

And he pounds into me, right there against the wall. I meet him thrust for thrust, jerk for jerk, and the sensations are insane. My muscles ache with the constant spasms. My skin feels like it cackles under the web of blitzing currents. My sex pulses in response to the sweet friction from his filling cock. I can't bear more and my body lets me know.

"Dayton, I'm close," I croak.

"Yes, me too," he grunts, and then I feel his cock lurch inside me.

"Ah, fuck!" he roars as he shoots his load inside me, his orgasm racking through his body.

He shakes with the effort of it, and I shake with him as his orgasm sparks mine again. And we both see a slice of heaven.

CHAPTER FOURTEEN

Dayton

DAYTON

The sound of a crash startles me awake. I jerk my head sideways, a little disoriented from being jarred so sharply from my sleep.

I squint my eyes against the glare of the sunlight streaking into the room from outside as I stare at Iris.

She stares right back at me as she pauses halfway into falling on her face. She is wearing the shorts she had on when she opened the door last night, and a white tank top. And a pained expression on her face as she grips her ankle in her hands.

"Are you trying to sneak out?" I ask, truly confused as to what exactly she is trying to do.

She stares at me for a second, looks down at her ankle, and then back at me.

"Of course not," she says. "This is *my* house."

I prop up on my elbows, a thread of amusement starting to wind itself through me.

"Exactly," I say.

She looks around the room like she's never seen it before. And then she turns back to me and nods. She releases her ankle, standing back on her two feet.

Her back goes up, and she clears her throat.

"Well, how about you start thinking about leaving then?" she asks.

My eyebrows jack up. "Rude, are we?"

She snorts, actually snorts.

"I am not *rude*. I just want my house back to myself. Surely you understand that," she says.

My eyes follow her as she walks—and tries not to limp—toward the dressing table in the opposite corner of the room.

"And what's that supposed to mean?" I ask.

She shrugs, keeping her back to me as she rummages with the contents on the dresser.

"Just that, you're a man, you know, and men have this natural innate fear of women being all up in their space. I'm just saying I feel the same way too."

She shrugs again.

My brows furrow as I realize she is not actually doing anything on the dresser, she's just fiddling.

The Iris I've known for these past few weeks doesn't fiddle. The word doesn't even relate with her.

I take the bedspread tangles around me off. I get down from the bed and pick up my pants from the edge of the bed. I start to get dressed.

"We should talk about last night, don't you think?" I ask.

Suddenly, Iris whirls around and stops short as she sees me. Her eyes widen slightly as they zero in on my chest. And then they start to trail down, and Iris does something else I have not known her to do—she blushes.

The necklace in her hands falls to the ground, and the sound of it hitting the floor startles us both out of the moment.

"Dammit," she whispers as she bends to pick up the necklace.

She turns around to place the necklace back on the dresser, and then she just stays like that. With her back to me.

"Iris," I call to her.

I want to see her eyes again. Those black eyes that enchant me.

Her shoulders rise and fall as she takes a deep breath. Finally, she turns to face me. She grips the edge of the dresser behind her.

She cocks her head to the side. "Hmm-hmm?"

I spread my hands out beside me. "Come on, let's talk about this," I say.

She stares at me for a while, and then she takes another deep breath, exhaling sharply.

"Fine. I know sex is off the table, and I know I'm the one who took it off. And I know I should have stopped it when we—"

"I was there too," I say, cutting in.

She looks at me. "Right. Well, I'm not going to apologize—"

"Do I look like I'm fishing for an apology?" I ask, cutting in again.

She gives me a look, obviously not pleased with the way I keep cutting in.

"So, now what?" she asks.

I shrug, the answer pretty obvious to me.

"We continue like this," I say.

I glance around the room, looking for shirt or any other piece of my clothing.

Iris snickers. "No, uh-uh," she shakes her head. "I took sex off the table for a reason," she says.

"You didn't tell me about this reason," I say, suddenly realizing I never even asked.

She gives me a look before turning away. She bends to pick something up from the side of the dresser, and when she straightens and stretches it out to me, I realize it's my shirt. I take it from her.

"Thanks."

I start to put the shirt on.

"Well?" I ask when she doesn't say anything.

She crosses her arms over her chest, and I feel my member harden at the sight of the hard tips of her nipples behind the tank top.

"I don't have to give you a reason. I don't even have to *have* a reason. I just want sex off the table, period." She gives me a challenging look. "If you don't like it, you can find someone else to be your celebrity girlfriend," she says and shrugs.

I look at her, at the wild mass of dark hair tumbling around her face, the challenging look in her eyes that intrigues me instead of whatever she had hoped to achieve by it.

I shrug too.

"Suit yourself. I'm just saying, it's going to be kind of hard now to ignore the sexual pull between us."

And I watch in amused fascination as only one of her eyebrows jack up, the other staying down. Her lips curl and the smirk on them surprisingly thrills me.

She tilts her hips to the side as she stares at me.

"Are you saying you absolutely cannot resist having sex with me, Dayton?" she asks.

I know a challenge when I hear one.

My own lips curl too as I stare right back at her.

"Oh *I* can. I'm only thinking of you, you horny horn bag," I say.

Those beautiful black eyes of hers narrow.

"*'Horny horn bag?'* What the hell even is that?"

I shrug again, strangely enjoying this exchange way too much.

"I said what I said," I pause, "*horn bag.*"

Iris chuckles lightly. "Oh, we'll see. We'll see who will not be able to keep it in his pants. That's right, I used *'he'*. I said what I said, *he,*" she says the last part in a whisper.

We stand in the middle of Iris's room, early in the morning, with the sun streaming in through the blinds and pieces of our clothing that we had discarded last night strewn every which way in every corner of the room, and stare at each other.

"I'm hungry," I say suddenly.

Iris doesn't blink. "I could eat," she pauses, "I could cook."

Surprise flitters through me, but I just nod.

She nods too before turning to walk out of the room. After a last glance around the room—*I don't even know where the hell my suit is*, I think to myself—I follow her out.

We walk into the living room, Iris to the kitchen space, which is behind the counter, and I to look around.

In the morning light, the room is now more visible than it was last night, and I am able to get a better feel about it. Not that I was particularly looking at the room last night; my mind had been elsewhere.

But now, as I look around at the tasteful looking furniture arranged in a semi circle around the slightly crowded living room space, I get a feel that is all Iris.

The room looks scattered, but I don't doubt she knows where everything is. Cut-out materials and sewing tools lay scattered all over a desk in the corner of the room facing the streets below. The throw pillows arranged on the sofa and chairs hold varying degrees of printed African art.

I raise my eyebrows as my eyes land on a little brown stuffed bear tucked in the corner of the sofa.

I hear sounds as Iris moves around in the kitchen behind me. I walk over to the sofa to pick the stuffed bear up and turn to face Iris.

"Was he here all night?" I ask.

Iris looks up from breaking eggs into a bowl; her eyes narrow slightly, and she flushes a little as she sees what I'm holding.

"He's a resident of this house, you're not. Put him down," she adds before going back to mixing the eggs.

I squeeze the bear lightly. "You mean to tell me he was watching us all night long?" I lay a hand on my chest, feigning shock. "Wow, you have a perverted Mr. Bear living with you, Iris."

She stops mixing and looks up at me.

"His name is Dwayne Rock," she says through gritted teeth. "Now, put him down."

I feel the corner of my lips tilting up. "A first *and* last name? Fancy."

I walk toward the kitchen area, stopping to place 'Dwayne' on one of the chairs facing the sofa. My brows furrow as I take my seat at one of the stools in the kitchenette.

"Wait, Dwayne Rock? As in Dwayne 'The Rock' Johnson?"

Iris looks at me from below her eyelashes as she pours the mixed egg into the skillet.

"Yeah, so?"

I chuckle. "Nothing. Just," I glance back at the bear, "he sure *looks* like a rock," I say, tongue in cheek.

Iris narrows her eyes at me again. "Bite me," she says.

I smile. "Already giving in, are you? Well, come here, let me indulge you."

"In your dreams, Pade," she says.

She flips the eggs, and the sound of the slight sizzle fills the room.

"Speaking of bosses...," she says and trails off.

I tilt my head. "Were we?"

She doesn't turn around to face me, just continues flipping the eggs.

"My boss called me in to her office a week ago, or five days ago, I guess. Anyway, she called me in and told me I will be presenting my designs at the company's mini-show next week."

She turns to face me, skillet in one hand and long spoon in another. She drops the skillet on the counter and takes out plates from a cupboard. And I realize she's avoiding my gaze.

She starts to pour scrambled eggs into the plates.

"And she let me know me getting the chance to present my designs is as a result of my new popularity," she pauses, "from dating you."

The toast maker dings, signaling the readiness of the toast bread. Iris takes the toast and puts it beside the eggs on the plates.

And she finally looks at me.

"She wanted something in return for granting me the opportunity of showcasing my designs. She wanted me to spy on you."

And I see.

I look at Iris as she looks back at me steadily.

"And are you?" I ask.

Something passes briefly through her eyes at my question, but it's gone just as quickly.

"I told her no. I'm telling you about it now because I don't bullshit."

Our gazes remain steady on each other. I nod.

"Good. Because I don't bullshit either. Which is probably why I can smell one from a mile away," I say.

The unspoken 'I don't smell any here' resonates loud and clear between us.

Iris nods too, and pushes a plate of eggs and toast toward me. She hands me a fork before taking one for herself and sits down on a stool on the other side of the counter.

I look at her a second more before looking down at my food.

"You know, I probably would have done the same in Lisa's shoes," I say, taking a forkful of eggs.

Iris nods. "I know. Like I told her, your job sucks too."

I chuckle. "Sometimes."

I glance back at the design materials strew all over the desk in the living room. The sunlight streams in through the window and lands on them, making them look like a heap of bright colorful mess.

I look back at Iris. "You've got this," I say.

She smiles at me. "Thanks."

Chapter Fifteen

Iris

IRIS

I tack the last pin on the sequin dress currently sitting pretty on a mannequin. I lean back to look at the dress. It's a dark green flowy number with tucks and creases all over the length of it with a sleeveless bodice and a sweetheart neckline.

"Maybe the pins are too much," I mutter to myself.

I tilt my head to the side a little, trying to see if I can see the dress in a different angle.

I worry my lower lip. The pins are probably not too much, and the sweetheart neckline is probably not too low. I'm probably just losing my shit.

I close my eyes and throw my head back a little.

"God, I hate myself," I mutter to myself again.

"Oh! Ooh, this is so beautiful," Alyssa croons as she walks into the dressing room, her eyes riveted on the dress.

"It is?" I ask, desperate for any form of validation.

Alyssa turns to look at down at me. I am on my knees as that is where I have been for hours, fussing over the dress.

"Are you kidding me? Of course, it is," she says.

"You're not just saying that to make me feel better, are you? You're not just saying that cause you're my friend," I say, shaking my head.

Alyssa smiles at me. She gets down to her knees beside me.

"I'm not. It's really beautiful," she says, looking up at the dress.

She looks back at me, and smiles. "I am so happy for you. And proud of you. What I would not give to be having this totally normal breakdown before a show."

I laugh. "Me losing my shit is totally normal," I say.

Alyssa laughs too. "It is."

She looks around the dressing room.

"Wow, this is totally mag."

I look around with her too. Even though we were always the ones preparing the showroom and taking care of the dresses to be shown every time before a show, we were never allowed inside the private dressing rooms that were reserved for the designers who were showing their designs.

But now I'm in one of the private dressing rooms.

"Yeah, it's crazy," I say as I look around the spacious room.

A workstation with company provided sewing materials, comprehensive ones, stands to one side in the room. A clothes rack with the other four designs I plan on showing arranged on them.

A makeup station for the models and a vanity table with a lighted mirror stand in another corner of the room. A long sofa with a light pink, soft, fur-like material placed over it is beside the vanity.

I look up at Alyssa as she stands up to walk to the workstation. She coos and gushes over the materials on it.

"So, who's around? Anyone from other companies yet?" I ask.

Alyssa, still mooning over the workstation, answer me absent-mindedly.

"Uh, yeah, Reese Sprite from YOUand Colin Stu from GLAM-OUR."

"Oh." I fiddle with the ends of the dress. "No one from VIVID?"

"No, not yet. But Lisa is already in the showroom, and all the senior designers too."

"Oh."

Alyssa finally seems to remember me; she turns away from admiring the workstation to face me.

"You are going to do great, I promise," she says.

I smile at her. "Thanks," I say.

"I have to go. You're the only designer not asking for this and that, you know," she chuckles lightly, inclining her head.

Because I do know how some designers can be mean and demanding, I nod my head.

"Yeah, I get it. Go. Thank you, Alyssa," I smile at her to let her know how grateful I am for her.

She smiles at me again before turning to leave the room.

Before I can be alone with my thoughts again, six models enter, chattering. They stop when they see me.

The one in front, a tall black lady about six feet with dark skin so smooth its flawless, smiles at me.

"Hey, Iris," she greets me.

I smile at all of them. "Hey, Breanna, ladies. Thank you for coming," I say.

As is ENAMORED's tradition, I was allowed to choose the models I want wearing my designs. And I had chosen these five. But I had chosen Breanna especially, for a unique reason.

"Okay, ladies, please take off the clothes on the rack and put them on. I want to see how they look on your gorgeous bodies before the show." I turn to the plus-size model amidst them. "Lana, the dress on the mannequin's yours. Thank you, ladies."

The models move to the rack and Lana to the mannequin.

"Breanna? Please, can you come with me?" I ask.

She turns toward me. "Sure."

I turn and walk toward the steam room, which is behind a small door in the dressing room. I push the door open, revealing a long pink dress with Celtic lace at the edges and center.

"This is *faisean*. That's Celtic for fashion." I turn to look at Breanna. "I remember there was a time we were talking and you told me your great-grandfather was Celtic. I'm part Irish, and I wanted to represent my culture in a way through my designs. I would like you to wear it," I say to her.

She smiles at me, then at the dress. "It is a beautiful dress. Really. And I would be honored to wear it."

She takes the hanger which the dress is hung on and walks toward the dressing room.

I turn to look at the models as they wear the clothes I designed. *My* designs. I feel a thrill run through me at the knowledge. I take a deep breath and place my hand on my stomach as a queasy feeling takes root in it. Pride warring with nerves.

My phone pings in my pocket; I take it out to read the message that just delivered. And I see it's from Dayton.

"You've got this."

That's all. 'You've got this,' that's all he writes.

And I smile as I remember his face in my kitchen a week ago, saying the exact same words to me.

The show manager sticks his head into the dressing room. "It's time!" He announces and leaves again.

I take a deep breath. "Okay, here we go," I mutter to myself.

I walk back into the dressing room.

***

Two hours later, and it's all over.

I stand by the buffet table with the three other designers who also presented their designs in the show.

Low slow music flows out of the speakers as the senior designers and guest designers from other companies mingle amongst themselves in the hall. Reese Sprite and Colin Stu chat with one of ENAMORED's senior designers, Lisa Banks. Marie Ferrell, a senior designer from VIVID, hugs Lisa Marion as the two women greet each other.

I feel my breath hitch a little at the sight. The two of them are my idols in design. They are designers I respect and worship, and I only hope my designs will ever be as good as theirs. And I am in the same room with both of them.

I follow Marie Ferrell's designs religiously, and I know of all the progress she has made in all her designs over the years. I can sight a Ferrell design from a mile away.

Beside me, another senior designer from YOUis talking to one of the other designers. And from the glow on her face, he apparently liked her designs. I look to my other side and see two senior designers from ENAMORED talking to the two other designers. One is grinning from ear to ear, the other looks like she's about to burst into tears.

"Oh God," I mutter to myself.

Just then, a woman sails up to me. She barely reaches my shoulder; her red hair bounces around her face in springy curls as she looks up at me.

"Iris Siobhan, right?" she asks in a feathery light voice that sounds musical.

I recognize her from the show. Grace Underwood. She is a senior designer from YOU, and Lisa Marion's third cousin. Alyssa—who had taken the role of researching all the guest designers upon herself—had whispered the cousin bit to me during the show.

"Yes, that's me," I say, already praying hard in my heart.

Her face—plump and flushed—lights up as she smiles at me.

"I really *loved* your designs. Especially that sequin dress? The own with the sweetheart neckline and tucks. I *loved* that one!"

My heart sings. I smile at her. "Thank you so much. It means a lot to me that you like it," I say to her.

She beams, actually beams, up at me. "And the real champagne problem was picking my favorite between the Irish gown and the yellow pantsuit."

Oh, my heart sings. "Thank you so much," I say again.

She takes both my hands in hers and squeezes them. She smiles at me and then moves on.

And just as she leaves, Marie Ferrell walks up to me. I hold the breath I was about to release, and then she smiles at me. She looks over at Grace, who is now talking to one of the other designers.

"She is delightful, isn't she?" she turns back to me. "And I happen to agree with her on the yellow pantsuit. That was a magnificent design. Well done."

She smiles at me again, and a part of my brain lets me know I need to say something.

"Thank you," I whisper, as the breath in my lungs suddenly isn't enough to make out coherent words.

She smiles at me again before moving away. I feel lightheaded as I watch her walk away.

And the feeling continues to be with me thirty minutes later as the last of the designers gives her remark on my designs.

My phone rings, and I dip my hand into my pocket to bring it out. I see Dayton's name scrawled across the screen. He wants to video-call.

I look around the hall; it's now emptying, leaving only a few of the junior designers and show managers around.

I walk out toward the back exit of the hall. As I step to the streets outside, I swipe on Dayton's call. I smile widely as his face winks on my screen.

"Hey," he says in a way of greeting. "The show's over, I take it? Marie told me. I didn't want to distract you by calling during the show."

I nod my head enthusiastically. "Yes, it's done. And I aced it, Dayton, I aced the bitch!"

I can feel myself almost vibrating with the happiness bubbling inside me.

Dayton just smiles at me. "Good," he says.

"I mean, I know their remarks are an informal gauge of how well our designs did. And the official score will come out later after the company's board meeting tomorrow. But," I take a deep breath, "you can always tell right from the remarks you get from the designers in the aftermath of the show. You can always tell when you've done good or bad. You can just always tell."

Dayton smiles at me, and I smile back, my heart singing again.

"And I did good, Dayton, I did good," I say.

"I believe you did too. Marie sounded impressed," Dayton says.

My eyes fill. "She did?"

Dayton nods. "And I never doubted you for a second. I told you, you got this."

I feel the tears in my eyes well up even more at the confident way in which Dayton talks. Like he truly had believed in me all this while.

I look up, and on a large billboard sign just across the street from where I'm standing, I see Carl's face plastered broadly on the screen. A new model on his arm.

His smirk does nothing to me as it would have a month ago.

I nod, my eyes still on the billboard even as I address Dayton.

"You know what, I'm starting to believe that too," I say.

I look back at Dayton and smile.

CHAPTER SIXTEEN

Dayton

I slap Brian's leg as I walk past him to take my seat in a chair adjacent to him.

"Get your feet off my table," I say, taking a swig of my beer.

We're in my house as Brian has come over to watch the basketball game. New York Knicks versus Los Angeles Lakers.

Brian puts his leg back up on the table.

I just roll my eyes as I lean back in my chair, deciding to let his childishness go.

"Love LA, but the Knicks rule all the way tonight," Brian says as he takes a swig of his beer.

"Fucking A," I agree, tipping my beer bottle toward the screen.

The sound of the game is the only sound between us for a while.

"Heard from Iris lately?" Brian suddenly asks.

My eyes still on the screen, I answer absentmindedly. "No, why?"

"Nothing."

We don't say anything again as our focus returns to the game. Or, at least mine does.

"She was really excited about her design show last week. She told me all about it when she came in to *A ghrá* the next day."

Thomas Bryant of the Lakers makes a driving dunk.

"Damn it!" I mutter.

Brian clicks his tongue. The screen shows Lakers fans celebrating, and then it swings back to the court.

"She also told me how you called her after the show, and told her you had believed in her right from the start," Brian says after a moment.

I sigh. I turn to look at him. "You here to watch the game, or gossip?" I ask snidely.

Brian just gives me a look. "There's something there, isn't there?" he asks.

I feel my pulse trip a bit as Brian looks at me steadily. I take a sip of my beer to cover my reaction to Brian's unnerving question.

"Of course there's something there. She's my very public girlfriend, there has to be something there for the press to be convinced, now, doesn't there?"

I turn back to the screen, hoping Brian drops it. Of course, he doesn't.

"You didn't have to call her though. Or tell her you believed in her," he says from behind me.

I sigh again, hanging my head. "I just called her, Brian. There's nothing more to it."

When Brian doesn't say anything, I turn to look at him. He looks right back at me with patient eyes.

"Fine," I pause, "I enjoy talking to her. We didn't start out as friends when we proceeded with our arrangement. But now, we are."

Brian stares at me for another second.

"She is a likeable woman," he says.

I scoff lightly. "She is. We've chatted this past week on the phone, and it's been great. I haven't gone to her house since last week though, neither has she come to mine. We," I pause and look over at Brian, "have a bet going. To see who'd give in first to the sexual tension between us."

Brian scoffs, and then he looks at me closely. "You're serious," he says.

"Yep," I take a swig of my beer.

Brian laughs. "Good luck with that," he says.

I give him a look. "Yeah, yeah. Now, can we?" I ask, pointing at the screen.

Brian shakes his head, chuckling. He inclines his head in acceptance.

Just then, RJ Barrett of the Knicks makes a 25-foot three-point jumper.

"Yes!" Brian and I shout in unison.

"That's what I'm talking about!" I cheer at the screen.

The stadium on screen goes wild with Knicks fans jubilating.

I turn to smile at Brian—he has a mile wide grin on his face too.

"Neither of us are driving tonight, so want another beer?" I ask Brian as I walk toward the small bar in the corner of the living room.

Brian drops his empty bottle on the table. "Why not?"

I take two bottles of beer from the bar and walk back toward Brian. I hand one over to him.

"Thanks," he says as he collects it.

I can feel his eyes follow me as I take my seat back on my chair.

"What now?" I ask without turning back.

"The party your mom throws for your dad's birthday every year, that's tomorrow, right?" Brian asks.

I take a swig of my beer. "Since you already know the answer to that, what's your point?"

"You know I'll not be able to attend this year. I've got my meeting with *A ghrá's*—"

"Investors," I finish for him. "Yeah, I know."

I take another swig of my beer, a deep one this time, as I think of going to my father's birthday party without Brian. He's always been the sole reason I am able to tolerate the whole evening.

"You're always miserable at the party, you know that," Brian continues.

I just grunt.

"Why don't you take Iris with you?"

I slowly turn to look at Brian.

"What?"

Brian shrugs. "Why not? You just said so yourself, you enjoy talking with her. She could be a friendly face."

My brows furrow as I think about it. "Yes, but I can't ask her to do that," I say.

"Why not?" Brian asks again. "You guys literally have a contract that legally binds her to accompany you to events. Your dad's party is an event."

"Yeah, but this is a family event. It's just—it's—" I stop talking because I realize I'm close to stammering.

I never stammer.

"Look, it's just weird, okay? I'll go by myself. I'm a big boy, I can handle an evening at my parent's."

Brian shrugs, taking a sip of beer.

"Suit yourself. I just know how miserable you get at these things, that's all," he says.

Two hours later, the game comes to an end, and Brian and I stand up to retire for the night.

We beat the Lakers 112 to their very close 110.

"They always were a worthy opponent," Brian comments as he walks past me to dump the empty beer bottles into the trash can.

I grunt in agreement.

Brian looks at me. "Call her."

He turns to walk toward the bedroom he uses whenever he comes over to my place.

I stare at his closed door for minutes after he closes it.

"Damn it," I mutter to myself as I pick up my phone from the table. I click on Iris's name in my list of contacts, and after a moment's hesitation, I dial.

She picks up on the second ring.

"Hello," she says.

Her voice sounds a little breathless, and I am thrust back to that night two weeks ago. When she had opened the door in her Thank God I'm Female shirt and said my name breathlessly. Just like now. And the desire that had slammed into me like a dunk shot.

I clear my throat, bringing myself back to the present.

"Hey," I frown up at the time on the clock right above my head. "You're up late," I comment.

"Yeah, I was watching the game," she says.

I scoff. I feel my lips curl in amusement. "Of course you were," I mutter.

"What?" she shouts a little.

Probably so I'd have a chance of hearing her over the noise coming from her side.

I hear her shout at someone to 'quiet down!' I hear laughter, and then she mutters a curse.

"Look, let me just step outside. These morons won't let me hear myself talk, much less hear you. Hold on," she adds.

I hear a rustle, some shuffling, a door opening. And then, quiet.

Iris sighs. "Sorry about that," she says. "My dumb friends from the apartment across the hall from mine came over to watch the game at my place. And they're a noisy bunch."

I smile. "It's okay. Brian's over at my place right now for the same purpose. He's a lot quieter though."

Iris laughs, and the sound of it coils around my gut. A low ball of heat comes alive in me.

"So," I hear a sound like she's sliding down a door, "you were watching the game too?"

I walk to the kitchen, switching on the lights as I walk in. I take a seat on one of the stools.

"Yeah."

"Let me guess, Lakers?"

"Knicks?" Iris asks at the same time.

There is silence on both sides for a second.

"Oh you—"

"Of course you—"

We both stop again.

My lips curve. "Whooped your ass," I say.

"Oh, bite me."

"Sore losers like yourself don't get even that pleasure," I taunt.

"I'm going to make you eat your words, Pade. I promise you," Iris threatens.

I laugh, and I feel that ball of heat in my gut uncoil to light threads of amusement.

"Actually," I say after I stop laughing, "I want to ask you a favour."

"Oh? Great start, Pade, really great start," she says, her voice saccharine sweet and coming through very clear with it over the phone.

I hang my head back as I stare up at the ceiling. "You're going to make me beg for this, aren't you?"

"Oh. You think there was any other way?"

I sigh. "Fine. Please," I say.

"Hmmm. Let's hear the favour first," she says.

"I want to take you to an event tomorrow. A family event. My father's birthday party."

Iris doesn't say anything for a while. And in the space of the silence, I start to realize just how much I now want her with me at the party.

"It would just be a small gathering. Family and friends. Mostly family, really." And then I wince as I realize that fact is maybe not my best selling point as it is probably the scariest. "There would be others, of course, who aren't family. That is, I mean to say—"

"I'll go," Iris says, cutting me off.

I blink. "You will," I say.

She takes a deep breath. "Yes. I'd like to go with you to your parent's party tomorrow night."

I release a breath I hadn't even known I was holding.

"Okay then. I'll, uh, I'll pick you up at 8:00," I say.

"Okay," she says.

A beat.

"Goodnight, Iris," I say.

A beat.

"Goodnight," she says.

I click off. And I sit and stare into nothing for minutes, before I finally stand up to go to bed.

***

The next morning, I stand beside my car as I wait for Iris to come down.

For some reason I can't fathom, my shirt is suddenly too tight around my neck. I put two fingers in the space between my shirt and my neck, pulling it down a bit. I shift on my feet and glance over at the entrance of Iris's apartment building. I look around at the people coming and going on the street, people entering and coming out of Iris's apartment building.

Why isn't she coming out? I wonder to myself.

And then she does. And I can't look away from her.

Underneath an unbuttoned long black coat, she's wearing a silver dress that stops at her knees. Glitter winks shyly on the gown as she moves, and the silver earrings that droop at her earlobes twinkle in tandem.

But what has me rooted to the spot is her face. Her rich black hair is curled in curly waves around her face, giving her a gypsy look. And her black as midnight eyes shine as they look right at me as she walks toward me.

A little silver purse swings at the tip of her fingers.

And I blurt out what I think should save me from saying something foolishly poetic.

"You should know better than to dangle a shiny purse like that on a New York street."

Iris stops in front of me. Her eyes narrow. She looks down at her purse, and then back at me.

"I know. This is not my first rodeo," she says, holding her hand up to show a clasp attaching both handles of the purse together.

She inclines her head at me.

"Now, are you going to tell me I look beautiful, Pade? Or not?" she asks.

And I feel my heart stutter.

"You are beautiful," I say to her, meaning it with all my heart.

CHAPTER SEVENTEEN

Iris

IRIS

M y heart stutters.

You are beautiful. Not 'You *look* beautiful.' *Are.*

And with that look in his eyes. Oh boy.

I smile. "Thank you," I say.

A light breeze blows, shifting the collar of Dayton's shirt a little. My eyes latch on the exposed skin of his neck under his coat, and my pulse picks up as I imagine running my hands all over him.

"Shall we?" I ask abruptly, my voice coming out almost like a squeak.

I clear my throat before walking to the other side of car. I get in just as Dayton does. We both fasten our seat belts, and Dayton pulls out onto the road.

I glance at him sideways. "So, what do I need to know before I meet your parents?"

He glances at me briefly before looking back at the road.

He shrugs. "Nothing much. It's my father's birthday party; my mother throws it for him every year. And don't worry, we'll be leaving early enough," he says.

I chuckle, "No, that's not what I meant. I meant, like, any embarrassing memory or moment from when you were a kid." When he doesn't say anything, I add, "They're your parents, I'm sure they've been keeping up with you in the news. So they'd know we've been 'dating' for a month now. I should know about your embarrassing moments," I say and smile at him.

Dayton glances at me again, a slight frown on his face.

"No, it's fine, it doesn't matter," he finally says.

My eyebrows jack up. "It doesn't?" I ask.

Dayton grips the steering wheel tighter. "It doesn't," he says flatly.

Okay, what? I think to myself. There's definitely something here, something he obviously doesn't want to talk about.

I let it go.

***

Twenty something minutes later, Dayton drives into a large compound with tended flowers and a sprawl of an impressive garden. He drives the car round the high water fountain in the middle and pulls up in front of a huge modern-day house. It stands up high and majestic under the night sky, and the porch lights, all on and bright, wash the exterior of the house in warm, welcoming light.

Dayton gets out of the car, and I follow suit. The sound of soft music wafts out of the house, and I can hear the distinctive sound of laughter and guests chattering.

Dayton comes around to my side and holds out his elbow.

"Shall we?" he asks, throwing my earlier question back at me.

I look up at the massive house and back at Dayton. I smile.

"Ready as I'll ever be," I say.

We walk toward the entrance of the house, and a butler greets us.

"Good evening, Frank," Dayton greets the man who looks just like a butler. Tall, thin, and groomed.

He bends slightly at the waist, and I only notice because I'm watching him.

"Good evening, sir," he smiles, slightly again, before turning to me. "Welcome, ma'am."

I smile at him as we walk into the house. In the entryway, another butler-looking person, a woman this time, takes our coats.

I curl my lip at Dayton as I look at him. "I kinda suspected you grew up rich, white boy, but butlers?"

Dayton just smiles down at me as he hands his coat to the butler.

There is a strain around his eyes now that wasn't there on the ride over, and I wonder why that is.

We walk into the house proper, and my mouth drops open. Because the impressive grounds and pruned gardens and large waterfall outside do not even have anything on the inside.

A glittering chandelier hangs down from a high ceiling and into a wide space that I don't think can be called *a* living room. Maybe *two* living rooms. Definitely *three* living rooms.

Guests stand around chattering and mingling while flutes of champagne are passed around on trays by serving butlers.

"Wow," I whisper as I look around the humongous house.

A gigantic piano sits in one corner of the room, and I realize as I see a man seated at it, the sound of music I had heard outside was live.

"Wow, Dayton, this is mega..." I trail off as I try to think of the word to describe it all, "...fancy," I finally say.

"Yeah," Dayton says, looking out at the room at large, "it is."

I look at him. "Can't believe you grew up here. It's like a freaking castle," I say.

My eyes go toward the long winding stairs at the other side of the room. Its journey starts at the base of the floor and up into...infinity, I guess, as I don't see the end of it from where I'm standing. Even peering up.

And then I realize we are still standing at the entrance of the room. I look up at Dayton as he just looks on at the party going on in front of us.

"Do you know any of these people?" I ask quietly, staring with him at the guests.

"I've probably met half of them at one business function or the other," he says.

"Oh," I say, at a loss for the right thing to say.

But before I can think too hard about that, a couple walks toward us. And I know they're a couple because they just look it. The man, a tall built man with strands of gray hair at both sides of his rich dark hair and a face that, even with a few feet between us, I can already tell is the older version of Dayton's. The strands of gray just make him even more formidable.

The woman, a smaller person in height and air of formidability, with almost completely gray hair and smiling eyes that twinkle as she walks toward us with her husband, smiles with her lips as they both stop in front of us.

"Dayton," she says.

Only his name, just like that, and I hear a host of emotions in that one word. Happiness, gratitude, longing, joy.

"Mother," Dayton replies.

And I hear a host of emotions in this one word too. Detachment, distance, coolness, duty.

And I watch as the light dies in her eyes.

The formidable man looks down at his petite wife, and his jaw locks almost indiscernibly as he looks at his son.

"Dayton," he says.

And in this word, I hear command, censure, control, and coolness.

I clear my throat, hoping to slice the tension with the sound.

Dayton's mother smiles a little at me, I smile back and look up at Dayton. I give him a light elbow jab when he just stares stonily ahead. He looks down at me and finally seems to remember his manners.

He clears his throat. "Father, Mother, Iris Siobhan. Iris, John and Tessa Pade, my parents," he introduces us in clipped tones.

I smile brightly at them, holding out my hand. "Hi, so nice to finally meet you," I say in my brightest voice. "Happy birthday, Mr. Pade. You have a lovely home, Mrs. Pade, truly magnificent."

Mrs. Pade takes my hand, smiling back at me, a little of that twinkle back in her eyes.

"Thank you so much. Call me Tessa, please," she says.

I smile at her. "Tessa," I say.

Mr. Pade takes my hand in a firm shake. "John," he says.

I smile at him too. "John it is," I say.

And it is not until now I soddenly remember gifts.

"Oh my God!" I look at John, and then at Tessa. "We didn't bring gifts. Oh my God, we didn't bring gifts," I turn to look at Dayton, horror in my voice.

"It's okay, darling. John already got his gift from Dayton," Tessa says.

I turn to look at her, she smiles softly at me.

"Oh." I look at Dayton.

"Your secretary delivered it this morning," John says, looking at Dayton. "Thank you," he adds when Dayton says nothing.

His secretary?

I look up at Dayton again, whose stony expression hasn't yielded even a bit since we started talking.

"Come!" Tessa suddenly says, very brightly, "I'm sure you'd like to meet some guests. We invited Mr. Thompson," she says to Dayton. "We saw on the news that you're trying to acquire his country club. Mr. Thompson's an old friend of your father's. Your father has been talking you up all night to him."

As Tessa talks, an eager look on her face, I realize she is desperately trying to please Dayton with the news.

I look up at Dayton. He looks at his mother, then his father, and his stony expression turns even stonier.

His jaw locks. He takes two flutes of champagne from a nearby server's tray. He hands one to me and drinks from the other.

"No, thanks," he says to his parents.

I sputter on the flute of champagne I had just put in my mouth at the directness of his refusal. I look at Tessa, and the eagerness on her face dies at Dayton's words.

John's eyes flash. "You—"

But Tessa puts a hand on his arm, stopping his words.

"It's okay, John. This is a party, *your* party. We shouldn't be talking about business anyway," she says.

She smiles again, obviously trying to go for bright again, but missing the mark with the strains around her eyes.

"We watched the game last night. Your team won. I'm sure that must have been exhilarating," Tessa says, smiling at Dayton.

Dayton says nothing and just drinks his champagne.

Beside me, I feel his muscles, which had been previously coiled with tension, relax a bit though.

One for Tessa, I think to myself.

John obviously thinks so too, because he relaxes his stance as well.

"Yes. Although I think the Lakers are really damn good too," he says.

He stops a server and takes two flutes of champagne from the tray, passing one to his wife.

I smile at him. "Lakers fan too?" I ask.

Dayton snorts, not so quietly, beside me. I glance at him, John does too and then he looks back at me.

"Sadly, I'm not much of a basketball fan. Baseball is my sport. But from what I watched last night, the Lakers play like a damn fine team," he says to me.

I grin. "Yes, sir, they do."

He smiles at me, and he suddenly doesn't look so formidable anymore. Just like a man who loves sports.

"A Lakers fan then," he comments.

"Yes, sir," I say again, "since before I could walk."

He laughs, and I see Dayton so clearly in him. I laugh too, liking him just for that.

Tessa smiles, and the tension that was present before seems to have dissipated completely.

Just then, the MC calls John and Tessa to the stage.

Tessa glances at the stage, and then back at us.

"Sorry, we have to go and give a speech now." She looks at Dayton, hope in her eyes. "Maybe you'd like to join us?" she asks.

And from the way she holds her breath, waiting for his answer, I can tell this is not the first time she's asking the question.

Dayton stares at her, and I see something pass in his eyes before he locks his jaw and smooths his face into a blank expression.

"No, thanks," he says, delivering a second rejection for the night.

The hope in Tessa's eyes shatters, and she nods a little.

"It's okay," she says, wringing her hands together.

John gives Dayton a look, and then he puts a hand around his wife's shoulders as they turn around.

Applause rings out as they walk toward the stage.

I look up at Dayton, he watches them go with a blank expression on his face.

There is so much hurt in here, I think to myself. And it hurt to watch.

I take a sip of my champagne as John and Tessa reach the stage. John collects the microphone from the MC and greets his guests.

CHAPTER EIGHTEEN

Dayton

I watch as my dad greets his guests and makes a joke to which everyone in the room laughs. He turns to my mom and compliments her, citing her as the most beautiful woman in the room. She smiles up at him, looking at him like he's the best thing to ever happen to her.

Probably is too, at that. Because even when the work had been all they had been consumed with, they had had time for each other. Even then.

I had been the only one who had never quite made that cut. There had been just enough time for everything else but me.

And now, standing down below while they talked up there, both smiling into each other's eyes, I feel just like the outsider I had always felt like growing up.

I down the rest of my champagne into my suddenly dry throat.

"And to our son," my dad says, raising his champagne flute toward me from across the room, "who has always been the light of our lives."

He and my mom wear twin smiles as they look at me.

The guests applaud, all of them turning to look at me. Iris applauds too beside me.

"I need some air," I say, turning to walk out of the room.

The applause falters, and as I walk toward the terrace doors, I can feel eyes on me, speculating.

Now they see me, I think bitterly to myself. A memory from twenty something years back flashes into my mind.

It had been one of my parents' numerous charity parties; I had been seven, maybe eight, years old. And I had stood in the middle of the room—this very same room—alone and in my little suit as guests, just like these ones, had mingled around me.

They hadn't seen me then. Not even my parents.

I walk out onto the terrace, placing my hands on the banister. I hear my father make another joke to cover up my abrupt leave.

I close my eyes and take a deep breath. The first real breath I had taken all night.

I hear footsteps behind me. Iris's jasmine perfume wafts around me.

I take a deep breath of that too.

She comes to stand beside me. We don't say anything for a while, just looking out at the starless night sky.

"You okay?" she finally asks.

"No," I say.

She nods, and doesn't anything again for a while.

"After the design show last week, after hearing important designers compliment my work and tell me choosing between two of my designs had been a champagne problem for them, I felt high."

She laughs softly. The curls of her hair bounce lightly beside her face, and I think to myself, for the second time tonight, how she is true beauty.

"I felt high, and it was a better feeling than a champagne-buzzed feeling. It was finally getting validation for a work I already knew I was good at, but also finally getting support from people I admired and respected."

She turns to me, a light breeze ruffles her hair, blowing the curls away to reveal more of her face.

She lays a hand over mine on the banister.

"I'm here with you, Dayton, giving you all the support you need," she says.

She looks up at me, her black eyes shining even blacker in the night.

"I'm not in our arrangement to get back at Carl anymore," she says, looking into my eyes.

I move closer to her, reducing the distance between us to just an inch between our bodies.

Her eyes remain steady on mine. I feel my pulse trip, and heat goes straight to my libido.

"What are you in it for then?" I whisper, my gaze now fastened on her lips.

Her tongue runs over them, leaving a moist sheen. My heart beats faster and the heat becomes a full flame.

I lean closer till my lips are the distance of a thin strand of hair from hers.

"We have to go," I say.

Her eyes, dark with desire, look up at me.

"Yes," she whispers.

***

Thirty minutes later, I pull up in front of my penthouse building. I turn the ignition of the car off and turn sideways to look at Iris.

She meets my gaze, and I say a silent prayer of thanks as I see the look of desire still in her eyes.

She hasn't changed her mind.

Even now, sitting in the car in front of my house, I can't say exactly how I got here. I know I drove, but my thoughts had definitely not been on driving.

After Iris's 'yes' on the terrace, all I had heard was the roaring of the blood rushing in my head. And getting here had been my priority, so I had driven like a maniac.

But even with how fast I had driven, the drive from my parents' had still been the longest of my life.

And now, I'm just grateful the desire is still there for Iris. Cause it sure as hell hasn't left me.

I feel my groin tighten as I watch Iris breathe heavily. Her breasts rise up and down, rising up above the dipped neckline of her gown. She takes her lower lip in her teeth, and my eyes go to her lips, dyed a bold red from her lipstick.

Suddenly, the car is too hot, and I hear my own harsh breathing loud and clear.

The blood roaring in my head roars even louder, my fingers itch to run through Iris's wild black hair spread out around her face in front of me.

I have never felt this strong a feeling for anyone in my life. Not even Melissa.

The strength of my reaction to her right now is a little bit scary.

I force myself to breathe easier and take a deep breath to regulate my heartbeat.

"Maybe we shouldn't," I say, my eyes steady on Iris's face.

Even as the words come out, I can't believe I'm saying them.

What do I do with all these pent-up feelings? If she agrees with me, what do I do with the blood roaring in my head?

Her eyes on me, Iris slowly shakes her head.

"No," she says.

Thank God, I think to myself.

And in a split second, we're on each other. Our lips fuse to each other in a mating lock. I push my tongue in to find hers as I bury my hand in her hair.

Iris moans into my mouth, and the wordless sound sends a ball of heat straight to my cock.

I pull her head closer to mine, wanting to dive deep into her and never find my way back.

I trail my hand down from her hair to her shoulder, the feel of her smooth skin beneath my hands intoxicating me.

Iris moans again, and then she lifts up from her seat and comes over to my side. I lean back in my seat as she settles herself over me, her legs on either side of my lap. Her hair falls forward to frame our faces, and in the space between us, I look into her dark eyes and the answering heat of desire in them fans the ball of desire in mine even hotter.

My eyes on hers, I put my hand under her dress and graze her panties lightly. I trail my fingers around the silk material to cup her mound.

Her eyes widen slightly as I find her wet and pulsing. She gasps softly as I trace my fingers slowly and lightly over her panties.

Her hands on my shoulders grip me tightly as she throws her head back.

"Ah!" she whispers even as she moans.

I use my other hand to bring her head back.

"I'm going to make you come right here, right now. I'm going to drive you crazy with my hands, baby," I whisper to Iris.

My hand still holding her head in place, I slip my fingers into her panties and cup her bare mound with my hand.

I moan deeply myself as I find her so wet already.

"You're so wet, baby, so ready for me, your juices are flowing all over my hand," I take my hand out of her panties.

I wriggle my fingers in front of her face, they glisten with her juice. My eyes on hers, I lick my fingers one by one.

Iris moans again, gyrating her hips against mine as she does so. Her eyes flame even hotter as she watches me lick her juices off of my fingers.

"I'm just getting started, baby," I say.

I return my hand back to underneath her gown. Slowly, I remove Iris's panties.

"Ready to come for me baby?" I ask.

As she starts to nod, I dip my fingers into her pussy and start to pound into her.

"Ah! Dayton!" Iris screams my name as she bounces up and down on my lap.

The wanton look of pleasure on her face and the force with which she screams my name goes to my head, giving me a dizzy feeling of rush.

"I'm going to come! Dayton!"

I only increase the tempo of my fingers. "Then come for me, baby," I growl into her ears.

And she comes violently with a hard jerk; her body vibrates and shakes with the force of it. And she spills her cum all over my hand.

We both breathe deeply for another minute, our labored breathing the only sound in the car.

I close my eyes and throw my head back on the headrest of my seat. And then I feel Iris's hand on my pants. She cups my cock through my trousers, her dark eyes on me.

"I can drive you wild too, Pade," she whispers.

And I realize she can, as my breaths start to come in pants. Her hands spread to caress my thighs, slowly and treacherously.

She leans in to me, running her tongue along the insides of my ear. My eyes roll back in my head as the overwhelming feeling of pleasure takes over me completely.

"Baby," I whisper, "you're killing me."

She leans away and smiles at me dangerously. "You ain't seen nothing yet."

She undoes my belt and dips my hand into my trousers. Her warm fingers wrap around my length and start stroking slowly.

"Baby," I groan.

"I'm just getting started," she says, and then increases the movement of her hand.

She strokes me faster, pumping my cock hard and with just enough pressure to make the pleasure start to build up in me.

I bury my fingers deep in her hair as the pleasure builds up even more. I stretch my legs, the pressure between them causing me to cast my eyes up.

"Oh, baby, I'm going to come," I growl.

She smiles at me all the while continuing to pump me up.

And for the third time tonight, I think how beautiful she is.

I take her face in my hand and kiss her. Thoroughly. Her hand movement doesn't slow down or falter.

And the orgasm tears through me like a rocket.

"Ah! Fuck! Oh God!" I close my eyes as I vibrate with the strength of the orgasm.

Iris cups me, taking all my cum in her hand.

When I finally come down from the high of the orgasm, and I open my eyes to look at Iris, I find her smiling at me.

She takes her hand, dripping with my cum, and puts it in her mouth, destroying me.

"Oh, baby," I groan as I pull her close to me and kiss her deeply.

After a while, we lean away from each other. I put my hands on Iris's hips to keep her in place as she tries to move. She smiles and looks around the car.

"We drove all the way from your parent's house without doing anything, and we couldn't just walk upstairs before jumping each other?"

I smile lazily. "What can I say? We're like rabbits."

She throws her head back, laughing.

Chapter Nineteen

Iris

IRIS

I open my eyes and look around at my surroundings. And this time, as my eyes land on the gray bedsheets wrapped around me and up at the picture of the smiling woman, I immediately know where I am.

I cast my mind back to the night before. After we had gotten out of the car, Dayton had asked me if I wanted him to drive me home. Or if I could just sleep over at his place.

He had asked casually, of course, but that still hadn't stopped the thrill from running through me.

I had chosen to sleep over at his place. If not anything, it's more efficient this way, I think to myself.

Dayton didn't have to drive all the way over to my place last night, and I had a really good night sleep in a really nice bed. Win-win.

I stand up from the bed and realize I'm in just my panties and bra. My lips curl as I remember. Oh yeah, we had had sex.

Just before we finally went to bed, Dayton had fucked me almost to oblivion.

It's a win-win-win.

I bend to pick up my gown from the floor and hear Dayton's voice from behind me.

"Now that's a sight," he says.

More like drawls, I think to myself as I stand up straight to face him and find him leaning lazily against the doorjamb.

My mind goes back to the first time we had had sex, to the morning after. This current scenario looks a lot like the morning after our first night together. Except this time, instead of a well-pressed shirt that made him look like a boss, he is wearing a gray sweatshirt that makes him look like the answer to every woman's morning after prayer.

"Haven't you got some place to be? Some company to buy? You *are* a CEO, you should be leading by example," I say, my voice dripping with sarcasm.

He tilts his head slightly to the side, his lips curl with amusement.

"I am a CEO, and I do have companies to buy, just not today. It's Sunday," he says.

It's Sunday?

I look at him watching me with a cocky look on his face.

"What, you religious?" I ask, trying to cover up the fact that I had forgotten today was Sunday.

"Not in the slightest," he says.

He pushes off the doorjamb and walks toward the same wardrobe like last time.

Why does this keep happening to me? With this man. Standing in my underwear while he looks like a fantasy or a boss or a mini god.

I start to put my gown on when he comes back in. He holds out a shirt to me. A female graphic tee.

One of my eyebrows go up as I look at the shirt, and then him.

"Why are you giving me this? I have my own clothes," I say raising up my gown.

"It's cold outside, you'll be a bit warmer in this than that," he says titling his head toward my gown.

I eye the shirt, and then him again, and then I take it from him.

"Besides, it would be more comfortable to wait in," he says just as he turns to walk away.

"To wait in? Why would I wait?" I ask.

He turns back. "There's been an accident. A twelve-car pile-up on 12th and 18th earlier this morning. Traffic is backed up for miles."

"What?" I say as I start to look around the room for my phone. "Where is my phone?" I ask no one in particular.

"It's on the bedside table," Dayton says, angling his head toward the little table beside the bed.

I walk toward it and take my phone from the table.

"When you're ready, come to the kitchen. I'm making us breakfast," he says and turns to walk away.

My eyebrows jack up at his back. I don't know which implication of Dayton's last statement I should address first. The fact that Dayton can *cook?* Or the fact that he's cooking breakfast for me?

One thing at a time, I think to myself. I look down at my phone as I switch it on. I instantly see from blogs and news channels that the 12-car pile-up was no joke.

"Only New York," I mutter as I scroll through articles and posts about the accident.

"Okay," I sigh, switching off my phone, having seen enough.

I look toward the bedroom door, thinking about Dayton making me breakfast in the kitchen.

I look down at the shirt in my hand, then up at the picture of the smiling woman above me.

"If this is yours, I'm sorry," I say to her.

She just continues smiling down at me. I sigh again.

"You know what? I'll wear both," I say to her. "Yeah," I start to put on my gown, "even I don't feel comfortable wearing your clothes," my gown halfway on my body, I peer out of my gown's sleeve hole to look up at the smiling woman. "Not that I'm saying this is your shirt. I mean, you never said it was yours."

I stop as I stare at the picture.

I finish straightening my gown, and I look up at the picture of the smiling woman again. "Which, of course, you could never say, seeing as you're a portrait." I pause, running my tongue over my teeth. "And I'm talking to a portrait."

I pull on the graphic tee over my gown.

"There. Not so bad now," I say, throwing down my hands beside me.

I walk toward the door, and turn to look at the portrait of the smiling woman one last time, before I walk out to the living room.

I turn toward the kitchen and walk in. Dayton turns at the kitchen counter to look at me.

One eyebrow jacks up at my dressing, but he doesn't say anything.

I take my seat on one of the stools at the counter.

"So, what's for breakfast?" I ask cheekily.

"Bacon and omelette. As he lists each item of food, he serves them, so now he places a full plate in front of me.

"Oh," he takes an apple from a fruit bowl on the counter and places it beside my plate, "and fruit."

My eyebrows jack up. "Nice," I concur.

He inclines his head, acknowledging me.

I look down at the food and then back up at him.

"This isn't weird for you?" I ask, genuinely curious.

Dayton glances back at me as he tidies up the countertop.

"As weird as you cooking for me the morning after at your place?" he counters back.

I roll my shoulders. "Yeah, I know. Just, I don't know, this just seems different, somehow. I mean, we're having breakfast together, after sleeping together," I say, looking at him pointedly. "That doesn't freak you out? It freaks most guys out."

He looks at me. "I'm not most guys," he says and sits down to eat. "Most people think having breakfast the morning after indicates some kind of intimacy. But this," he waves his fork between us, "is not intimate. We're just passing time until they clear the pile-up on the road and I can take you home."

I nod and take a forkful of omelette. And I'm pleasantly surprised at how good it tastes.

"This is really good," I say.

Dayton just grunts as he continues his breakfast.

"I'm surprised you can cook. Most CEOs don't cook," I say.

"And how many CEOs do you know?" Dayton asks, his lips curled slightly.

I take his joke, I smile. "Touché," I say.

Dayton chuckles. "I don't do it often, but I like to cook. I did a lot of my cooking when I was a kid," he says.

My fork pauses halfway to my mouth. Dayton continues eating, and I realize he doesn't know he just revealed a very personal detail of his life to me.

I glance at the door joining the kitchen and the bedroom, thinking of the portrait of the smiling woman. I admit, that's one personal detail I am very curious about.

But I look back at Dayton, and talking about a woman that had probably meant so much to him that he still hangs her portrait up on his wall, is probably too heavy for a breakfast story.

Besides, there seems to be something in his childhood that warrants talking about. Cooking his own meals when he was a kid?

I look at his bent head as he focuses on his food, and something squeezes at my heart.

The memory of the tension between Dayton and his parents yesterday night comes flashing through my mind.

I take a bite of bacon. "So, I really enjoyed meeting your parents last night," I say studying him.

His fork falters a little on the way to his mouth, but he recovers smoothly.

And then, as I realize what my statement sounded like, I rush to clarify. "I mean, I know you didn't take me there to *meet* your parents, you know. Not like we're dating for real like that. I mean, we have a contract and all—"

Dayton looks up at me. "We have a contract for business events only, not personal or family. Me inviting you to my dad's party, that was just..." He trails off as he obviously tries to think of the correct way to put whatever he wants to say. And then he looks at me. "My mom throws a party for my dad every year, and I and Brian usually go together. He wasn't able to yesterday because he had a meeting."

He stops, looks away from me and then back at me again. "I guess I just want to say thank you, for going with me."

It takes me a minute to find my voice. "You're welcome," I finally say.

He nods, and then turns back to his food.

I play around with mine for a while. "Why do you not like going to your parent's events alone?" I ask.

I stare at the mop of his black hair as he doesn't look up.

"I don't mean to pry, and you don't have to tell me if you'd rather not, but I noticed the tension between you and your parents."

He continues to stare down at his food, but then he raises his head up to look at me.

"We're just not close," he says, his face blank of any expression.

I nod; I know when a man is putting up walls. I'm surprised to be a little hurt by it though, I realize, as I feel a sharp little pain through my heart. I turn back to my food, and we don't say anything for a while.

"I don't know them," Dayton finally says.

I look up at him; he stares into space blankly.

"They were never around much when I was growing up, so I barely know them."

He shrugs, and I realize he doesn't know how sad everything he's saying is. It's just reality to him.

"And now they want to get to know me."

"And you don't want to?" I ask gently.

He looks at me. "I can't," he says.

I open my mouth to say something, but he cuts me off.

"I just can't. Okay?"

I look at him, and then I nod.

We continue eating, and for a while there's just the sounds of our forks hitting our plates. And I realize even the silence is comfortable.

"You lost the bet," Dayton suddenly says.

My brows furrow. "What bet?"

He stops eating, and I look up to find him staring at me, a smirk on his face.

And then I remember. And I remember saying 'no' when Dayton had said we should stop.

I close my eyes. "Damn it," I whisper.

I open my eyes to find Dayton grinning.

"You know what, breakfast in the morning after *is* an intimate affair," he says, propping his elbows on the table and leaning toward me. "An intimate affair to win a bet in," he finishes.

He laughs as I throw my apple at his head.

CHAPTER TWENTY

Dayton

DAYTON

"Hey, man, what's up?"

I nod at Brian by the bar and take my seat on one of the stools lined around the counter.

The pub gives an airy feel as just a few patrons are scattered around, most of them lounging relaxingly while either nursing a beer or watching a rerun of a baseball game on the T.V. in the top corner of the pub.

Some of them are doing both.

"Slow afternoon?" I ask as Brian places a bottle of beer in front of me.

"Well, it is Sunday afternoon. Most people take Sunday afternoons as a mini vacation and stay in with someone. Speaking of, why are you not with Iris?"

Brian frowns at me as he cleans a glass cup with a rag.

I frown right back. Seeing as I am just coming back from dropping Iris off at her place.

"Why would I be with Iris?" I ask, taking a swig of my beer.

"Uh, I don't know, cause today is her birthday?"

I frown again, because this is definitely news to me.

"Today is her birthday?"

One of Brian's eyebrows jack up. "You didn't know?" he asks.

I put my bottle of beer to my lips. I don't know if I'm using it to avoid answering Brian's question, or if I'm using it to tamp down on the surprising disappointing feeling suddenly rising up in me.

We had been together most of the morning—having just dropped her off thirty minutes ago—after being together all night. And she hadn't said anything to me.

And I sound like a needy woman.

I take another swig of my beer, this time, in disgust.

"No, I didn't. Our relationship's a fake one, remember?"

Brian continues studying me as he cleans yet another glass.

"Oh, I remember," he pauses, "do you?"

I frown up at him; he just gives me a look before walking away to attend to a customer.

I look down on my bottle of beer as I wait for the disappointed feeling in me to settle or slide away.

I ease a hip up to take my phone out of my pocket. I put it on and my fingers hover over Iris's name for a minute. I finally click on it and type a message.

Happy birthday...

I stare at the screen of my phone, at the words that suddenly don't quite feel accurate enough anymore.

Just then, Brian walks back up to my side.

"You know, she had a small get-together here last year for her birth-day. Just her and a few of her friends. Maybe she'll do that again this year," he says.

He lifts his shoulder in a shrug before walking away again.

I look down at my phone's screen again, at the words. I erase them and stand up from my stool, my mind made up on what I want to do.

I walk toward the door, signalling to Brian as I get to the entrance.

"Could you reserve the pub for a private party?" I look down at my wristwatch; 10 o'clock. "At 12 o'clock," I add.

Brian smiles. "You got it."

I open the doors of the pub and walk outside.

***

Two hours later, *A ghrá* bustles with people, conversations, laugh-ter, music, and drinks.

An upbeat Irish song plays now, its rich melodies sounding out of the speakers. A group of men, fifty-ish and sixty-ish in their ages, raise their cups of beer in salute to the music. They also let out a collective loud cheer.

The men are regular patrons of *A grhá*, and they were part of the few that had been hanging around the pub when I had come in this morning. Iris's friend, Alyssa, had advised me to invite them or else they would be pissed at me if I didn't. Apparently, they were friends of Iris, and she loved hearing stories about Ireland from them.

I take a drink of my own beer. Alyssa was the only friend of Iris I knew, and so she had been the first one I called when I had decided to throw a surprise birthday party for Iris. And now, looking out at the room full of people, I know Alyssa is definitely not her only friend. She has made more friends in New York during the last two years she's been living here than I have in all the years I've been living here. Which is all my life, save for my years in college.

More laughter rings out in the room. Conversations between people mingling amongst themselves continue progressively.

I take a drink of my beer again as I watch the room from the counter at the bar.

My gaze lands on another group of people, a young mid-twenties group of two men and three women. Iris's neighbors. The loud ones who had been watching the game in her room the night I had called her to accompany me to my family's dinner party.

Just then, a slim brunette with a bottle of beer in her hand walks up to me. Alyssa. She smiles up at me as she takes the seat opposite mine.

"You got them all here," she says.

"You are the one who knows all the people here, and how to get to them. Thanks, by the way," I add.

She smiles again. "You're welcome. But even though, yes, you don't know any of these people, you were still the orchestrator of this whole thing. So, it's all on you," she says.

I don't say anything, cause, well, what is there to say?

Alyssa tilts her head slightly to the side, her eyes studying me.

"This is a really good thing you did for her. She's going to love it. The surprise, the people, the thought behind it, everything," she says. When I don't say anything again, she adds, "You really know her. This," she uses her free hand to encompass the room, "this is the type of thing that gets to her."

I shift a little on my stool, finding myself uncomfortable with the way Alyssa seems to be sure I know Iris so well.

"Well, I mean, who doesn't like this type of thing, right?" I ask rhetorically.

Alyssa just smiles again as she takes up her bottle of beer and tips it toward me. I pick up mine and hold it to hers.

"To Iris, an amazing woman we both know," she says.

I look steadily at her, and then I clink my bottle against hers.

"To Iris," I concur.

We both drink from our bottles.

Brian walks up to us, smiles at me, then Alyssa.

"Refill?" he asks.

"No, I'm good," I say.

"It's my best friend's party, and it's an open bar...so yeah, another for me," Alyssa says.

Brian laughs. "Coming right up," he says before leaving to get her order.

Just then, we both look over at the group of older men I had noticed earlier. Now joined by a couple of around the same age.

"I hope we did the right thing inviting Iris's parents," Alyssa says, her gaze still on the couple.

The man raises his bottle of beer as he laughs at something one of the other men said. The woman laughs just as hard too. They both seem to be having a good time.

"Why? Is she not close with them?" I ask Alyssa.

She turns to looks at me. "Oh, no, they're close. Daniel and Cara Siobhan are two of the best people I know, and great parents. But, it's just weird, you know? Having your parents at your birthday party, don't you think? She would want to get drunk and have the time of her life. And she can't do that with her parents here, you know?"

I frown. "Yeah, I guess I see that."

"But it's fine though," Alyssa says with a shrug. "They'll probably retire early anyway."

I nod. "So, Iris is on her way?" I ask.

I had given Alyssa the task of getting Iris here.

Alyssa swallows her drink before replying. "Yeah. I didn't bother to be covert about it, seeing as today's her birthday, and she'd definitely put two and two together when I called her to come out." She shrugs. "Only thing is, she'd probably suspect a dinner with me and some of our other mutual friends. What she doesn't know is that she has a full party instead."

Alyssa pauses and smiles at me again. "You know, with the status of you guys' relationship, I never really expected much. But, now, I think there's something more here between you and Iris. You probably don't know it, Iris definitely doesn't, but I do. Doing all this for her has nothing to do with business, and everything to do with heart."

Alyssa smiles again and takes the bottle of beer Brian places in front of her. She smiles at Brian before walking away to mingle in the party.

"You know, she's not wrong," Brian says beside me.

I give Brian a look. "Of course you would think that," I say dryly.

I take a swig of my beer though to hide my discomfort, cause Alyssa's words had left an uncomfortable feeling in me.

"Whatever, dude," Brian counters with his own dry tone. "But seriously, this is really nice," he says.

"Why does everybody keep saying that? It's just a party in a bar."

"For some people, like Iris, that's all it takes. Friends, family, party, music, and open bar."

"Should have just bought her a damn necklace," I mutter to myself.

Brian laughs, and then his gaze shifts to the entrance of the pub.

"And here comes the birthday girl," he says.

He taps on the bell he had placed above the bar to get everyone's attention. I turn just like everyone else toward the entrance.

Iris steps inside the pub, and shouts of 'Surprise!' goes up in perfect tandem.

She jerks, startled, and the distracted frown on her face turns to shock. She actually turns to look behind her, before turning back again to look at the crowd of people gathered. And then when she starts to look at each familiar face, realization dawns on her face.

She lifts a hand to her mouth as her eyes goes from one person to the next. Even from where I'm sitting, I see the sheen of tears form in her eyes as Alyssa walks up to her to hug her.

I feel a slight twitch in my chest as she is passed from the arms of one person to the another. Each of them saying 'Happy Birthday' and adding some comment or the other.

"A damn good thing," Brian says behind me before walking toward where Iris stands.

I watch him hug her, and she hug him right back. She laughs at something he says, that dazed look still on her face.

Just then, her eyes meet mine from across the room. The room fades away as we stare at each other. Different emotions pass through in her eyes, filled with the sheen of tears, sparkling under the lights of the pub.

At that moment, someone else pulls her into a hug, breaking the eye contact. I pick up my bottle of beer and drink from it to wet my suddenly dry throat.

Someone starts to sing the birthday song, and the whole party crowd takes it up. Iris laughs as her neighbors make silly hand gestures as they sing along.

As the song winds down, Iris looks around the room.

"You guys! You are amazing, all of you. Thank you for this, this is the best birthday ever. Thank you, guys!" she shouts over the noise in the bar.

One of the fifty-something men raises his cup of beer. "Here's to a fine proper lass! Slàinte!" he shouts.

And others join in, raising their bottles and cups of beer.

"Slàinte!" they all cheer.

Somebody else turns the music up and another of the fifty-something men takes Iris's hand, pulling her to the dance floor.

I hear Iris's laughter clearly from across the room.

CHAPTER TWENTY-ONE

Iris ♥

"Good night, Jed," I say as I close the cab door.

"One step closer to the grave, lass. Enjoy every moment of life. Like me!"

I laugh as Jed looks up at me from inside the cab with droopy eyes. He is most definitely drunk, I think to myself. I stare at him affectionately, my heart all warmed up from having the best night ever.

Just then, Jack Rowe and Ronan O'Brien snuggle up to Jed, their eyes equally droopy as they all look up at me.

"You are a pretty lass, aye, a pretty one," Jack drawls, ever the charmer.

I smile at him. "Thank you, Jack."

Ronan smacks Jack awkwardly on his arm. "She is smarter than she is beautiful. Brains take precedence over beauty, for sure," he says, his words slurring.

Jack snorts. "Shows what you know about women," he mutters.

Jed shrugs both men off of him, and that starts up a drunken pushing rustle between the three men.

I peer into the front seat of the cab, and my eyes meet Brian's. He gives me a wry, amused look.

"I'm only at peace because I know you'll get them home safely," I say to him. "Get them home safely, will you? Please," I add.

Brian just smiles his easy smile. "I've got this. It's just three drunk men," he says.

Jed, Jack, and Ronan all turn to look at him.

"Hey!" they all slur in unison.

Brian and I both chuckle.

"I've got this," Brian says again. He looks at me. "He's up on the roof. And whether he knows it or not, he's waiting for you."

I look back at Brian. He doesn't have to say his name for me to know who he's talking about.

"Go," Brian says.

He winks at me before giving a nod to the cab driver. The car pulls away from the front of *A ghrá* and onto the streets.

I stay where I am for another minute before walking back to the pub.

The pub is almost empty, with just a few of Brian's bartenders left, cleaning up. I look around and wince at the party mess lying around, chairs and tables haphazardly strewn all over the room.

I turn to look at Sven, one of the bartenders, behind the counter, and the one in charge when Brian isn't around.

"This must be a nightmare. I am so sorry for," I use my hands to encompass the pub, "all of it," I finish.

Sven, a tall guy with faded beach blonde hair and a smooth baby face, smiles easily at me. Dimples wink at the side of his cheeks.

"It's the job. Brian wouldn't mind if we come in early tomorrow to clean up, but we kind of prefer to do it tonight," he says, referring to himself and the two other bartenders in the pub with him.

"Okay, well, I'm going up to the roof...," I trail off, knowing I don't have to explain to him.

"Okay. I'll leave the back door open for you when we leave," he says.

"Thanks, Sven," I say, smiling at him.

He smiles back. "No problem. Happy birthday, Iris."

"Thank you." I smile. "Goodnight," I say as I turn to walk toward, and up, the stairs in the backroom that lead up to the roof.

The night breeze hits me instantly as I step onto the roof. My heart starts to pound loudly in my chest as my eyes land on Dayton. He is seated on a park bench.

As if he senses my presence, he turns to look at me. And my pulse escalates as his eyes lock with mine.

"Hey," I say, mildly surprised my voice comes out sounding so steady.

"Hey," he says back after a moment. "Everybody get off okay?" he asks.

"Yeah. My parents left a while ago, and Alyssa followed Ryan home. Ryan...he's one of my neighbors. He and Alyssa have this on-again off-again thing going on. She uses any slight booze situation as an excuse to hook up with him," I say, waving it off. "Brian took the three musketeers home." At Dayton's bland gaze, I start to explain who the three musketeers are. "The three musketeers, they're—"

"Jed, Jack, and Ronan," Dayton says, cutting me off. "Yeah, I know them. Kinda hard to miss them."

I don't know what to make of Dayton's bland tone of voice, but I catch a glimpse of his lips twitching at the sides. I smile to myself.

I walk toward him to sit beside him on the bench. And then we both stare out at the night, not saying anything.

"I don't know why I didn't tell you today was my birthday," I begin, breaking the silence.

I feel Dayton shrug beside me. "You didn't have to," he says.

I nod. "Maybe not. But I wish I did," I say, looking at him sideways.

He turns to look at me too. I feel a frisson run through me just at the same time a breeze blows by.

But I know the frisson is not from the cold.

I turn back to staring at the lights below; Dayton does too.

There is silence again.

"Did you like having your parents around tonight?" Dayton asks.

I turn to look at him, my brows furrowing a little at the odd question.

"Yes, very much. Why?" I ask.

"Alyssa wasn't really sure if it was a good idea. She felt they would hinder you from getting drunk and having the time of your life."

I smile. "Of course she did. I think Alyssa's just projecting her fantasy on me though."

"So you didn't want to get drunk and have the time of your life?"

My smile stretches wider. "Well, sure, maybe," I pause as I think about it. "But I didn't really want to," I finally say.

"Why not?" Dayton asks.

I turn to find his eyes on my face, steady and intense.

"Because I wanted to be doing something else," I say, my eyes steady right back on his.

The memory of our eyes meeting when I had entered *A ghrá* earlier tonight pops into my head. It had felt like the whole pub had disappeared, and it was just us two.

And now, the shining lights of New York City don't exist for me anymore. Nothing does. Not while I'm staring into Dayton's eyes.

And that thought scares the living shit out of me, so I break off the contact. I turn to look away from Dayton.

"There's just something about rooftops, isn't there?" Dayton suddenly asks.

My lips curve. "There sure is." I pause. "It's like the whole world is laid out at your feet, and because it's down there, it can't touch you."

"And when you think about the sad things, they don't feel so overwhelming."

I turn to look at the side view of his face.

What sad thing are you thinking about? I think to myself. *And how can I make it go away?*

I turn back to stare forward again, my heart aching.

"Thank you," I whisper after a while.

As Dayton turns to look at me, I turn to look at him too.

"Thank you for tonight," I say, meaning it with all my heart.

"You're welcome. It was clear as day that you bring joy to the lives of everyone at the party tonight. And they celebrated you for it. No one is more deserving."

I feel a tight squeeze around my heart as Dayton's words wash over me.

"I couldn't help but think, seeing the pub filled with people you've made friends with, that I don't make friends." Dayton turns to stare out at the city lights again. "I meet people every day, and some of them are interesting people, interesting enough. But I don't make friends with them." He pauses. "It doesn't take a shrink to know that that is somehow tied to my childhood, and being all alone up till I was ten years old and Brian and Patrick and Melissa came to live in my house."

He falls silent again, and I don't say anything. I wait patiently for him to say what's on his mind, and I tuck away my curiosity about who Melissa is for now.

"They're trying to reach me. I see their efforts and their hope. But I just can't seem to find a way to let them in," Dayton says.

He doesn't have to say their names for me to know he's talking about his parents.

I lay my hand on his. We both look down at the contact, and then we both look up into each other's eyes.

"You matter to them. Let that thought be with you the next time you see them. That's how you let them in," I say.

We stare at each other for a while, and then I lean in and place my lips gently on his.

I close my eyes as another breeze blows by, and I feel something settle in my heart.

CHAPTER TWENTY-TWO

Dayton

DAYTON

"Of course you invited her to come with us," I say looking at Brian.

He shrugs. "What? I thought you would be happy. I mean, ever since her birthday party a week ago, a surprise party that *you* threw for her, by the way, you guys have been, well, real chummy," Brain says.

I give him a look. "'Chummy?' How have we been chummy?"

Brian gives me a look right back. "Really? You want me to spell it out? Make us both uncomfortable?"

I shrug. "Spell what out? There's nothing to spell out, as far as I'm concerned," I say.

Brian gives me a steady look. "The long eye contact, the high school kids 'hellos' you both use to greet each other. The staring at the other when the other is not watching." He pauses. "Do you need me to go on?"

"You're seeing things," I say stubbornly.

"Oh, come on, everyone around you guys can see it. Only the two of you actually involved don't." He pauses, and his tone turns serious. "You should tell her about Melissa," he says.

I look at him. "No."

When Brian just continues to give me a steady look, I sigh. "Look, I threw her a surprise birthday party, to which I invited all her friends and her family. Of course she was grateful to me, and maybe that gratitude results into some lingering stares, sometimes. But that's it. That's all." I give Brian a look. "Now come off it, will you?"

Brian throws his hands up in surrender.

"Fine. But she's still invited to come with us to my Dad's. It's *my* birthday, and she's my friend. And I want my friend there."

"Uh huh," I say, not believing his reason for one minute.

Just then, the bell above the entrance to *A ghrá* chimes, and we both turn to look over at who just entered. I feel my heart skip a beat as Iris steps in, and before I even realize I'm doing it, my lips curve into a smile.

When hers curve in response, I realize I'm smiling at her like an idiot. I school my features back, hoping I look like a normal human being now.

She walks toward where I'm seated, and Brian is standing beside me.

Her long, flowy dark hair is let down, and it frames her face in a mass of curly waves. She is wearing a yellow sundress, and as the flowy material swirls around her knees as she walks, I can tell the material is of a very light texture.

Little lavender flowers are printed all across the sundress. The sleeveless nature of the dress leaves her arms bare, and the rich creamy skin of her arms looks all soft and smooth.

On her feet are black strappy sandals, and the bareness of her open toes incite a little rush through me.

I clear my throat and force my gaze back up to her face as she reaches Brian and I.

She smiles, and I'm sure this is the first time I'm actually dazzled by someone. Her black eyes light up with her smile, and I find myself staring into them.

She stares back, and the contact is only broken when someone clears his throat behind Iris, indicating she is blocking his path.

"Oh, sorry," she says to the stranger. She turns back to me. "Hi," she says.

"Hi," I reply.

Brian clears his throat. "Hello," he says.

We both turn to look at him, and I wince as I suddenly realize I had just done the very thing I denied ever doing, just a few minutes ago.

"You two better go get ready. We leave for my dad's in two hours," Brian says before walking away to attend to his customers.

"Oh God, oh God, oh God," Iris repeats beside me as soon as Brian leaves.

I turn to look at her. "What's wrong?"

The distress on her face is evident.

"I haven't gotten Brian a gift," she says.

"Oh. Well, I'm sure it'll be fine. Brian is not really that hyped up on presents anyway."

"That doesn't mean I won't get him anything." She looks at me. "Have you gotten him a present?"

"Yeah," I say.

"Oh, God, don't tell me your secretary is going to send this one too," she says. And then immediately slaps both her hands over her mouth, her eyes wide open in shock.

She shakes her head, clearly alarmed at herself. "I am so sorry, that was out of line. *Way* out of line. I'm so sorry," she says again.

My brows furrow in confusion. *Maybe I can forgive her if I know what the hell she's talking about*, I think to myself.

"Wait, why would you say my secretary—" I trail off as it clicks for me.

"I am so sorry, I didn't mean to imply anything by that careless comment. Honest," I say.

"It's fine. Of course you would think that, you know, since I had done it in your presence before." I pause. "But my secretary doesn't have anything to do with Brian's gift. I picked it out myself. Actually," I glance at the time on my wristwatch, "I should go pick it up right now. I could pick it up on our way to Coney Island, but I think he would guess what it is from seeing the shop where it's from."

I stand up from my stool as I talk; Iris lays a hand on my arm. My skin warms at the cool contact of her fingers.

"Can I come with? Please? Maybe I'll get an idea of what to get for him from this shop."

"Oh," I say, thinking about it.

Spending more time than I have to all weekend, with Iris. Alone.

I look at her, at her big black eyes, and I feel a tug in my chest.

Yeah, that's not catastrophic at all, I think to myself.

"Yeah, sure," I say.

"Oh, thank you so much!" she says, gripping my forearm again.

I look down at her hand on my arm, she looks at it too. We both look up into each other's eyes.

I know what I'm seeing in those black eyes of hers. Acceptance.

Even though I'd never admit it to Brian, ever, he was right. Ever since the night on the roof, after Iris's birthday, and we had shared that kiss, something had changed between the two of us.

Being the businessman that I am, I study people and their body language when it comes to drawing up a contract with them. Because I know how important knowing my business associate is.

And ever since that night on the roof, something had changed between Iris and myself. Like our dynamic had shifted somehow. To something more, more real. A fact to which I get the feeling Iris is okay with.

And which, strangely, I find I am too.

But something's holding me back.

"We should get going," I say abruptly.

Iris nods, her gaze on me.

"Yeah, okay," she says.

I turn to walk toward *A ghrá*'s entrance, Iris following behind.

"Hey, we're going out for a bit. We'll be back soon," I call to Brian on our way out.

Brian throws his hands up. "Really? Right now? We have less than two hours before we have to be on the road, the two of you," he says.

"Calm down, Mom," I say wryly, and Iris chuckles beside me. Brian just gives us both a look. "We'll be back soon," I say again.

I open the door to let Iris go out before me; I follow her.

Once we're outside, I walk toward my car parked right outside *A ghrá*.

"Oh, is the shop far from here?" Iris asks.

I turn back to look at her. "Well, no, not really," I answer.

"Why don't we walk instead then?" she asks.

My brows furrow, the concept of walking as foreign to me, a native New Yorker, as Africa is to America.

"I'm sorry, did you say walk? Like we should walk all the way to the shop?" I ask again to verify.

Iris's lips twitch. "Yes. Afraid you'll stain your fancy shoes?"

I look down at my sandals, and my brows furrow even more. And then I look up to find Iris smiling, her eyes clearly laughing at me.

I give her a look. I look at my car, and then the street.

"But, why can't we just take my car? It's faster," I say, completely perplexed by the whole walking idea.

Iris walks up to stand in front of me.

"Come on, just try it. And if you don't like it, we can take the bus," she says.

My eyebrows arch higher. "The bus," I say.

Iris laughs, and the musical lilt of it fails to please me this time around.

"Come on, rich boy," she says.

She starts walking away from *A ghrá* and down the street. I look back at my car, and then her, at my car again, and back to her.

"Oh, for God's sake," I mutter before hurrying to catch up to her.

We walked, and we talked. And I realize I had never enjoyed myself more than I do walking with Iris to the shop.

I don't even realize we have gotten there until Iris stops walking and points up at the storefront.

"FORM, isn't it?" she asks.

I look up at the shop, and my brows furrow as I realize we've gotten to our destination.

"Yeah," I say absently, staring up at the shop like I had never seen it before in my life.

Iris chuckles at the perplexed look on my face.

"And we got here in one piece," she says. "Well, except for seeing the rare sight of a man running across the street, naked, and almost getting run over by a teenage delivery boy on his bike," she smiles up at me, "we got here in one piece."

I find myself chuckling too. "Yeah, I guess we did," I concur.

Iris smiles. Before she can push open the door to the shop, someone else opens the door, coming out. We both enter.

The overhead lights of the shop glare brightly as we step in.

Men's wristwatches and cufflinks and other accessories lay on display glasses all around the shop. All of them expensive looking.

There are few browsers in the shop, most of them women searching for the perfect gifts for their men.

Just then, one of the attendants walks up to us, smiling.

"Mr. Pade, welcome back." She turns to Iris, her smile in place. "Welcome, Mrs. Pade, I'm Shonda."

My eyebrows arch up. Iris looks up at me, and then back at Shonda; she shakes her head.

"Oh, no, no, we're not together. I mean, we're together, to-geth—like, dating together, but not—"

I draw the attention of the confused Shonda back to me.

"She's my girlfriend," I say simply.

Out of the corner of my eye, I see Iris's head whip up to look at me.

Shonda blinks. "Oh, okay. I'm so sorry for the mistake," she says.

"It's fine. Do you have it?" I ask.

Her face schooled back into a polite mask, Shonda nods.

"Yes. Please, this way," she says and turns to walk away.

I take Iris's hand in mine and follow Shonda.

Shonda takes us into a private showing room, goes straight to a cabinet in the room, and brings out Brian's gift. She opens the clasp on the black ornate box, brings out a brown leather wristband with gloved hands, and turns it slowly from side to side, showing Brian's name engraved intricately on it.

"Wow. It's beautiful," Iris whispers as she looks at the band. She looks up at me and smiles. "And you had it customized just for him."

I shrug. "Yeah, well," I say, leaving it at that.

"You took really great care with Brian's gift."

She doesn't say it, but I hear the rest of the sentence. *Unlike with your father's.*

I look down at her. "He matters," I say simply.

Chapter Twenty-Three

Iris

"And he was just naked?" Brian asks, laughing.

"As naked as the day he was born, except with more hair. Oh God, the hair," I say.

Brian and I bursts into laughter; Dayton just smiles.

We are on our way to Coney Island, where Brian's dad lives. Brian is at the wheel while Dayton sits beside him in the passenger's seat.

I am recounting the story of the naked man that had run across the road on our walk to the shop.

And I realize Dayton's mood seems to get more broody as we drive farther from New York and closer to Coney Island.

I catch Brian's quick glance at Dayton, but he says nothing.

"Wait, you said he passed in front of you. Like, you were walking?" Brian asks, glancing back at me.

"Yeah," I reply.

Brian lets out a short laugh, and I see Dayton through the side view mirror as he rolls his eyes.

"Dayton walked? How did you manage that?" Brian asks between fits of laughter.

I smile. "It was like I was speaking Greek when I suggested it to him," I say.

"I just don't see why you would rather walk than take a faster, and more comfortable, ride," Dayton says dryly.

"Bet you liked it though," I say, leaning toward his seat and smiling at him. "He didn't even notice we had gotten to our destination until I told him," I say to Brian.

Brian laughs again. "Man, I would have loved to see that."

I smile, Dayton just ignores Brian. A few minutes later, Brian winds down a path leading up to a house.

"Home sweet home," he says with a little smile curving around his lips.

I follow his eyes to see a Victorian-style house with faded gray paint and a few short steps leading down from the porch.

Dayton shifts uncomfortably in his seat as Brian pulls up in front of the house.

Brian turns the ignition of the car off, and we all get out. The sound of beach waves crashing against each other draws my attention, and I turn back to see the beach a few feet down from the house.

"God, I love the beach," I say with feeling as I watch the waves.

A handful of people are littered around the bank of the beach, some in bikinis and beach shorts, lounging on lounge chairs, their faces to the sun, and some strolling or running around on the sand.

Brian comes to stand beside me; he lays a hand round my shoulder and looks out at the beach with me.

"I feel you," he says. He grins widely. "Welcome to my dad's house, Iris," he says.

I smile up at him. "Again, thank you for inviting me. I'm really honored," I say.

He smiles back down at me. "You're my friend, and I want you here to celebrate my birthday with me."

I tighten my arm which I had looped around his waist a bit.

"Well, I can already tell the next three days are going to be amazing. I mean, it's the beach!" I say pointing toward the waves.

Brian laughs. "It is indeed. Even though tomorrow is my birthday, I already feel blessed having you and Dayton here with me."

My heart warms. "I am honored to be here. You are one of the best people I know," I say.

Brian squeezes me to his side a little before letting me go.

He turns around to walk to the house. I give the beach one last wistful look before following him.

Dayton already has my overnight bag and his and is walking up the porch steps. I follow the two men up the steps. The porch is lined with several pots of brightly colored flowers.

Just as Dayton lifts his hand to knock, the door opens and a man fills the doorway.

A tall man, standing just a few inches shorter than Dayton, with clear gray eyes that warm at the sight of Dayton and Brian, smiles at me. A few gray strands in rich black hair, the man can only be Patrick Campbell with his resemblance to Brian.

"Welcome," he says in a voice that sounds almost musical with a rich Irish lilting brogue.

"Patrick," Dayton says in a way of greeting.

The two men hug, and not the side hug common to men these days either, but a full clasp with pats on both their backs.

They separate, and Patrick turns to Brian.

"Dad," Brian says.

And then the hug again between the two men.

Finally, he turns to me, and his warm eyes twinkle with welcome.

"Iris," he says my name before I can talk.

I blink, a little surprised he knows me.

"Uh, yes, Iris Siobhan," I confirm.

His eyebrows arch up as he studies me interestingly.

"Siobhan. You're Irish," he says.

And even though I know he's not actually asking, more like stating, I nod my head.

"Yes, I am," I say.

Patrick's gray eyes twinkle even more as he smiles. He turns to look at Dayton.

"How could you leave out the fact that she's a proper Irish lass, boy?" he asks, indignation rich in his tone.

Dayton hunches his shoulders—actually hunches—and looks chastised as he looks back at Patrick.

In the months I've known Dayton, I've never seen him hunch at someone's tone at him, much less of have a chastised look on his face.

And here he is, displaying both at the same time. *Wow*, I think to myself.

A warm feeling passes through me as I realize something else. Dayton talked about me to Patrick. He talked about me to a man he clearly respects, and sees as a father.

I look at him; he glances away from me, obviously uncomfortable by the knowledge himself.

"Sorry, I didn't know being an Irish lass was a big story," he says, a smirk in his tone.

Brian snickers beside him, clearly enjoying the exchange.

Patrick just gives him a look before turning to Dayton again.

"You take that sass out of your tone, boy." He turns to me and takes both my hands in his. "A fine, proper Irish lass, aye," he says, giving me a steady look.

I find myself enjoying his reaction to my heritage, so I smile back.

"You know your roots, girl?" he asks.

"I never forget," I reply, my eyes steady on his.

His gray eyes warm even more with appreciation.

"Aye, that's a damn fine answer," he says.

"Cool. Can we go in now, or do we stand outside all day?" Dayton asks dryly.

"Didn't I tell you to take that sass out?" Patrick asks Dayton.

Dayton just shrugs and opens the door and goes into the house.

Patrick's censure obviously doesn't bother him, I notice. Neither does it bother Brian, as he follows Dayton in too.

Patrick sighs. "Never could drum a whole lot of respect into those two," he says.

I smile. "Oh, you know they respect you. It's just their jobs as your sons to rile you up now and then," I say.

Patrick looks at me for a moment and smiles.

"You are a good person," he says simply.

And I know I have just received the highest compliment ever. My heart warms, and I smile back.

Patrick takes me into his home.

***

Hours later, at 7:30 p.m., we sit around the dining table, a spread of food between us.

I am seated beside Dayton, with Patrick at the head of the table and to my left. Brian is seated on the other side of the table, facing me.

"This is quite a spread, Patrick," I say, using his name as he had insisted on it earlier on.

I look at the bowl of mashed potatoes, roasted chicken quarters, plate of corned beef, bowl of rice and green peas, all spread out over the table.

"Thank you for welcoming me into your home, and for this delicious meal you prepared. It all smells heavenly," I say.

Patrick smiles, beaming with pleasure.

"Thank you," he says. "I like cooking, especially when I have a reason to. And when my boys come home, with a beautiful lady in tow, that's more than enough reason to take out the skillet." He pauses. "Dig in," he says to me.

Brian and Dayton had already dug in, already dismantling the heap of food on their plates.

Patrick sighs. "Of course, these two boneheads know nothing about it," he says.

Brian and Patrick lift up their heads simultaneously.

"Hey!" they both say.

I laugh. I pick up my fork and dig in too.

I close my eyes as the tasty flavors of the food burst in my mouth.

"Oh, Patrick!" I say, turning to him.

He smiles, eyes twinkling with pleasure.

"This is amazing!" I say between forkfuls of food.

"Thank you," Patrick says, smiling. "Now, tell me about yourself, Iris," he says.

So I do.

CHAPTER TWENTY-FOUR

Dayton

DAYTON

I open the door and step out to the porch. I look toward the beach, my eyes searching for Iris's dark hair among the sea of heads moving about on the beach.

The afternoon sun is already sweltering with heat, but its glare remains at the perfect temperature for sunbathing.

The waves of the beach crash against each other, adding its sound to the multitude of people's activities.

I sight Iris's face as she lifts it up toward the sun. She is lying on a lounge chair, the picture of utter relaxation as she arches her back a little.

Looking like that, back arched and face to the sky, she looks like she's trying to absorb the sun into herself.

I climb down the short porch steps and make my way to her. I stop beside her chair, and one look at her creamy smooth skin instantly has my heart rate up.

She has on a pink bikini, and the top bra doesn't completely cover her creamy breasts. And the soft swell of them as she breathes softly jacks up my pulse. The blend of color on the bikini is made so that the bold pink color also looks red at the same time.

She squints up at me, black sunglasses covering her eyes.

"Dayton?"

I find my voice. "Hey," I say.

I put my hands in the pockets of my shorts as they start to itch to run over the smooth plane of her long legs, all stretched out on the chair.

"What's up?" Iris asks.

And I realize I had just been standing and staring at her like a fool.

I clear my throat and look toward the beach, registering the other people around.

Men, women, some coupled up, some single. Children running around and obviously having the time of their lives.

Their carefree laughter balances out the itch in my fingers and the tension already lodged in the back of my neck.

God, you'd think I'd never seen a woman in a bikini before.

I turn back toward Iris. "I just got a call from Karen, my head of PR, and she told me DISH figured out where we were. Well, where *I* am, actually."

"DISH?" Iris asks.

"They're a gossip tv show that like to parade themselves as a journalistic one," I say, flicking my wrist in a 'not important' gesture.

"Oh, okay," Iris nods. "So what do we do?"

"We need to give them an interview. One of their reporters—and I use that term lightly—is on her way as we speak," I say.

I rub a hand over the back of my neck, already feeling the ball of tension lodged there as a result of Karen's call a few minutes ago.

I hate gossip tv shows, but I hate DISH more. And now I have to endure an hour of answering stupid questions and pretending to care about any of it. Because according to Karen, it's good PR for the uplifting image of myself we're trying to build.

Sometimes I hate my job.

"Oh, okay, sure," Iris says, starting to rise up from her chair.

My eyebrows arch up. "Wait, just like that? You're going to do it?"

Iris stands to her feet and looks up at me. Salty sand fragrance from her body hits my nose, and it smells like the moment after a long downpour of rain shower. Like petrichor.

I resist taking a deep breath. Barely.

"Of course. We have an arrangement, remember?"

The arrangement. Right.

"And besides, since Karen was the one who called you, I'm sure the interview must be good press for you, right?"

"Well, yeah," I say.

She smiles up at me and pats my chest lightly.

"Just let me go and change, huh?"

She picks up the novel she had been reading from the chair and starts to walk back toward the house.

I stare at her for another minute, and the way her hips sway beneath the tiny strap of bikini leaves me feeling appreciative.

I turn back toward the beach, contemplating diving in. The cold is not such a bad idea right about now, I think to myself.

***

I give the camera stand, and the baleful-looking man behind it, a glare.

"You're going to give Carlos nightmares, babe," Iris says.

I turn to look at her beside me; her lips are curved slightly as her eyes twinkle with amusement.

She had changed into a flowery dress that reminds me of summer with its flirty frills at her knees. Her hair is packed up in a high messy ponytail with a few strands left out to fall around her face.

And of course she had learned the name of DISH's cameraman.

"I think that's his goal actually," a throaty voice says.

Iris and I turn to look at the owner. Sanleya. Just Sanleya. And it belonged to the relentless DISH reporter. Apparently, she had joined her first and last name together, and had been using the conjunction for forever.

Her black hair, similarly raven to Iris's but stretched straight, falls down her back. She is a tall woman who towers over Carlos the cameraman, with an impressively fit body. Her bloodred lips curve as she looks at me.

"Let's just get this over with," I say.

There is no love lost between Sanleya and I.

"Yes, let's," she concurs.

She takes her seat on a set chair, facing the set chairs Iris and I are seated on.

She signals to Carlos, silently counts down from three with her fingers, and smiles widely as she hits one.

"Dayton Pade, Iris Siobhan, so pleased to have you on DISH. Thank you so much for granting us this time for an interview."

Disgust rolls inside me at Sanleya's phony smile. We all know there hadn't been a choice since Sanleya had called Karen and revealed she had found out I am in Coney Island, with Iris. And she had succinctly let it slip that she could share that information with dozens of other magazines and press unless we granted her an exclusive interview.

Today is Brian's birthday, no way I'm letting news mongers ruin it for him.

I incline my head slightly. "No worries. Happy to be here," I say.

I'm perfectly aware of how the game is played.

Sanleya turns her bright smile on Iris.

"This must be some romantic getaway, isn't it? The two of you, here, alone," Sanleya says, her eyebrows jiggling suggestively.

I answer her unasked question. "It is a personal trip, and Iris and I would very much appreciate our privacy on it," I say.

Iris and I alone in Coney Island is exactly what I want the story to read. I don't want to drag Brian and Patrick into the mix.

I can tell from the almost inscrutable twitch beside Sanleya's eye that she doesn't like my answer. But she smiles anyway. I smile too.

"Of course, definitely," she says.

She turns to Iris again, angling her body into a relaxed posture, no doubt to come off friendly.

"Girl, I love your hair, never could tame my curls. Had to go straight," she says, smiling at Iris.

I glance over at Iris. Before Sanleya and her crew had gotten here, I had given Iris some pointers, some diplomatic answers that she could give. And even though this is her first interview, you couldn't prove it by her right now. She sits, looking comfortable in her chair, with no air of nervousness around her.

My heart swells with pride, and I don't know when my lips curve in a smile.

Iris returns Sanleya's smile. "Thank you. I actually never tamed it," she says.

The straight answer gives Sanleya pause, and I can almost see her try to regroup.

She laughs, and it's as phony as her smile.

"I hear you, girl," she says. And then she changes tactics. "The news about your debut show at ENAMORED is all over the news. Congratulations."

Iris smiles, her face lighting up with pleasure.

"Thank you," she says to Sanleya.

"Seemed like everyone was impressed with your designs. Lisa Marion even gave you a special shout out in the interview she did for one of our episodes. Which will be out next fall."

Iris's eyes go wide with surprise. She turns to me, and then looks back at Sanleya.

"She did?" Iris asks.

"It's one of the special highlights in the episode. You heard it here first," Sanleya says with a half-smile for Iris.

Iris laughs shortly, obviously pleased with the news.

My heart swells with pride again. I take Iris's hand in mine; she looks at me.

"Never doubted her for a second," I say steadily to Sanleya.

Sanleya nods, giving me a steady look back.

"Yes, I can see that," she says.

She refocuses her eyes to the camera directly in her line of sight.

"We still have here with us New York's dream couple of the business world. Stay tuned, DISH lovers, we'll be right back."

Chapter Twenty-Five

Iris

IRIS

"**D**ISH lovers, we're back! And we still have here with us Dayton Pade, and the woman who won his heart, Iris Siobhan."

Really? Not only is the line corny, it's a little confining. Is all I am the 'woman who won Dayton's heart'?

But I just smile at Sanleya. I know the game, or at least I'm starting to get the gist.

I look at the Amazon-looking reporter in front of me. Sanleya. Her bold red lips just seem to make her mercury colored top and her black power pants even more daring.

Like the combination of the outfit wasn't already daunting on its own.

She smiles, and the word 'feral' comes to mind.

"So, how about a little dish? And, this is not me, I promise."

She laughs a little, holding up red painted fingernails the same color as her lipstick.

"But our viewers, the DISH lovers would love to know." She pauses and looks between myself and Dayton. "Do we hear wedding bells?"

Beside me, Dayton goes stiff. I glance at him, and I see his jaw set in a hard lock. A muscle twitches in his jaw as he looks at Sanleya with a hardened gaze.

But the bold reporter doesn't seem to notice as she continues on.

"I mean, you guys have been hearing what the tabloids are saying about you, right? Because it's all over New York. And you guys seem to have some very dedicated followers."

I look over at Dayton again. Ever since we had gotten to Patrick's house yesterday, I hadn't checked my socials. Not like I was very active on them before.

But I don't know if Dayton had checked, if he knew about the tabloids.

From the way he grinds his teeth now, I'm thinking not.

I lay a hand over his, willing him to release his tightly bunched fist. I smile at Sanleya as she looks between Dayton and I, a suspicious glint in her eyes.

"Honestly, we haven't paid much attention to the news lately. Like Dayton said earlier, we are here for some personal business. And there just simply hasn't been time for the outside world."

I glance at Dayton again.

"And as to the possibility of wedding bells any time soon, or never," I shrug, "you know there's not going to be an answer to that. Love with that kind of pressure is not love at all. Not anymore. And what we have, Dayton and I," I squeeze his hand beneath mine, "what we have doesn't need that."

Sanleya doesn't say anything for a while. Dayton looks over at me, and my pulse trips at the intense look in his eyes.

I can feel Sanleya's gaze between us.

"Well, you heard it here first, DISH lovers, these two lovebirds are in the lavender haze, and they don't plan on leaving any time soon. Keep rooting for #DAYRIS, DISH lovers, and we might just get that good news soon enough."

***

Few minutes later, I enter the kitchen, go straight to the refrigerator, and take out a bottle of water. I take a deep drink of the chilled water before closing the cap back on the bottle.

I stay as I am for another minute as I look out the small kitchen window. The beach spreads even to this corner of the house. But the waves of the beach are not what have my attention.

The marked grave beneath a gazebo is.

I look around the kitchen; no one is around, and the silent house indicates there's no one in the whole house too.

I drop my half-empty bottle of water on the kitchen counter and walk toward the screen door of the kitchen. I open the door and step out to the terrace behind the house.

I walk down the short steps; I steal a glance at the house behind me. I suddenly feel like I'm doing something bad.

And the feeling only intensifies as I get closer to the grave.

I step on to the hardwood floor of the gazebo after a slight hesitation. Hydrangeas, lilies, tulips, and lavender flowers adorn the interior of the small house, giving it a lively feeling despite the presence of a grave.

I look down at the grave, at the marble headstone on which words are carved.

"Here lies Melissa Campbell, the light, the star, and the joy of our lives. 1993 – 2020."

I wrap my arms around my shoulders as a light breeze blows by me.

Silently, I stare down at the grave, wondering about its inhabitant.

I don't know how long I had been standing like that when I hear footsteps behind me. I turn around, and my whole body jerks as I am startled to find Patrick behind me.

His gray eyes look at me steadily.

"I am so sorry, I didn't mean to—"

Patrick walks up to join me in the gazebo.

"Here, put this on, it's chilly out here," he says.

And only then do I notice he's holding a gray wool sweater in his hands.

I take it from him, trying to figure out his mood as I stare at his face.

As I put on the sweater, Patrick stands beside me, facing the grave.

"Stop looking at me like that, lass, or you'll bore holes into me," he says.

And in the confines of the small building, his voice seems to resonate even more deeply.

He turns his head to look at me, and his lips curve with a small smile, warming his gray eyes.

"If I didn't want people coming here to meet my girl, I would have laid her to rest elsewhere. So, relax," he says.

He turns back to looking down at the grave, and I try to take his advice to relax.

"The magazine people are gone?" he asks.

I nod. "Yes, they left a while ago. Dayton's on the phone with Karen."

Somewhere.

Patrick nods his head, and we both don't say anything for a while.

"She was never meant to be hidden. Not while she was here, and certainly not while she's not."

He smiles again, but this time, it doesn't quite reach his eyes.

He points at the headstone. "Those words, they're the truest I've ever written. She was my light, *our* light," he corrects. "Our star and joy. That was the only way my Melissa knew how to live."

He doesn't say anything for a while again, and I don't either. We both stare at the grave in silence.

"There are people in this world who feel, more deeply than others. There is a lot of hurt in this world, and while you and I have learned to balance the good with the bad, some people feel the bad too intricately to separate it. My baby girl was one of those people."

He pauses, and I swallow the lump that has gathered in my throat at the raw emotion in his voice. His Irish brogue is more pronounced now.

"And seeing that much hurt just broke her. She sometimes saw her ability to feel so much as a weakness, but she was the strongest person I knew. I was humbled to be her father."

Patrick keeps his gaze down, focused on the grave. And I know he's trying to pull himself together.

"It would have been an honor to have known her," I say, meaning every word.

There is obviously a lot of love, and respect, here for Melissa. The pain shows it all.

Patrick looks at me, his gray eyes warm with pleasure again.

"Aye. She would have liked you; you lasses would have been friends. This I know."

Another high praise, I think to myself. I feel my eyes water, tears threatening to fall behind them.

"There is more life to live. Give him that life, so that you might give *each other* that life," Patrick says.

I look into his eyes, steady on mine. And then we both turn as we hear footsteps behind us.

Dayton.

My heart picks up automatically as my eyes land on him. Our eyes lock, and I find I can't seem to look away from his gaze.

I don't know when Patrick leaves my side, but I watch his retreating back as he walks away. He pats Dayton on his arm as he passes by him.

Dayton's gaze doesn't leave mine, even as he walks up to stand beside me under the gazebo. In front of the grave of a woman he had loved.

We stand side by side, looking down at Melissa's grave, much like I and Patrick had done earlier.

We don't say anything for a while, and the silence is comfortable.

"She was the love of my life," Dayton suddenly says.

I feel those tears prickle behind my eyes again.

"I know," I say.

And then he turns to me. I look up into his eyes, and my heart skips a beat at the steady way he looks at me.

"I care about you," he says.

And my heart takes flight at the words. I feel the tears fighting to fall.

"I know," I say again.

Chapter Twenty-Six

Dayton

DAYTON

I drive through the gates, round the waterfall and ease the car to a stop in front of the house. I turn off the ignition and get out of the car. I walk toward the stairs, not even noticing that the flowers decorating the compound are in full bloom.

The dark cloud that always seems to hang over my head anytime I come to my parents' house is already starting to overshadow everything else.

I walk up the stairs to stand in front of the huge front door.

I look up at the door. It had always seemed larger than life to me when I was young. Sometimes, I had thought that maybe it was because I was so small, that maybe when I become older—bigger—it wouldn't look so daunting.

Now, standing in front of it years later, I realize my theory was way off.

Resisting the urge to ring the bell, I push the door open and step in.

I look around the foyer and there is no sign of Frank, the doorman, or of the housekeepers usually about, doing something.

And standing there, with the silence all around me, I am transported back to when I was young. Seven years old.

***

Flashback.

I skip down the long, winding stairs in my little tuxedo. I climb down from the last step to the foyer and look around the empty room.

"Frank?" I call out for the new doorman that had just started work last week.

No answer.

"Mom? Dad?"

No answer.

A bad feeling in my stomach starts to replace the happiness I had been feeling ever since my parents told me finally that I didn't have to stay in my room tonight, that I could join their party.

Even though it was just for one hour because of my bedtime, I am still very happy about it.

I walk slowly away from the foyer. As I get nearer to the living room, I hear sounds of muted music playing. I walk close till I'm standing on the threshold between the living room and the foyer.

Grownups dressed in fancy dresses and tuxes like mine stand around in groups. Some of them are laughing, some of them are just talking.

I see Mary, one of our housekeepers, carrying a tray with drinks on it and walking between the people. She is wearing a white shirt and black pants. And then I see our other housekeepers too, dressed like Mary and carrying trays too.

Nobody seems to notice me as I stand at the entrance.

My eyes scan the room, trying to find my parents. Just then, a woman turns her head and sees me. She taps the arm of the man beside her and murmurs something to him. The man looks at me and turns to walk away.

The woman continues to stare at me, and she has a look on her face. The kind of look Mary gives me when my parents don't come home for dinner and I have to sit at the dining table by myself, having my dinner alone.

The man comes back with my mom beside him. They stop when they see me. My mom pats the man's arm before walking toward me.

She has on a long, flowy black gown, and her hair is all piled on top of her head. She has makeup on, and even though I like it, I like her face without it better.

She smiles at me, and I smile back, happy to see a familiar face. She crouches down in front of me and runs her hand down my arm.

"You look so handsome, baby," she says to me.

"You look beautiful," I say to her, happy that she looks happy to see me.

She smiles, her eyes twinkling under the bright lights.

"Thank you, baby," she says.

She casts a glance at the people around us. I look around too, and it is then I notice that more people than the man and woman earlier are now staring at me.

My mom runs a hand over my hair, and I get that bad feeling in my stomach again at the look in her eyes.

"I'm so sorry, honey, I know I said you could come down tonight, but your dad and I received an unexpected guest tonight. And we have to impress him," she says.

A panicky feeling runs through me as I realize she is about to say I have to go back to my room.

"I'll be good," I say to her, ready to promise anything that stops her from making me go back upstairs.

"Oh, honey, of course I know you'll be good. You're a good boy," she says and kisses me on my forehead. She leans back and looks at me again. "But he is a very important guest, sweetie, and your dad and I need to put all our focus on impressing him. And you can't be roaming about on your own. I'll tell Mary to come and take you back to your room, okay? You can have anything you want, anything at all. Even your favorite, rocky road ice cream. Just ask Mary. Okay, sweetheart?"

She kisses me on my forehead again and smiles at me before standing up and walking away.

I stay where I am until Mary walks up to me. She smiles and that 'look' is on her face again as she takes my hand and leads me away from the party.

As we leave, my eyes catch my dad in a group of other men. I watch him laugh at something one of the men said just as I walk out of the room.

***

I blink as I pull myself back to the present. I haven't had a flashback to my childhood like that in years. And I don't need a shrink to know that it's because I had suppressed all my childhood memories.

Just then, my mom walks into the foyer. She stops as she sees me; her face breaks into a smile. And unlike my memory of her in the flashback, her face is bare of makeup, and a few wrinkles that hadn't been there before are now present.

And she still looks beautiful.

"Dayton," she says in welcome.

She walks toward me, and her peach-colored gown swirls around her with each step. She stops in front of me, and I can feel her palpable urge to hug me. And for the first time in years, I find I want to give her that.

But I can't seem to make my arms move.

"Mom," I say back to her.

My stiff tone doesn't dim the light in her eyes.

"Your father and I are so happy you decided to come," she says.

Every Tuesday, Thursday, and Sunday night for the past couple of years, my mom calls to invite me over for dinner. And every Tuesday, Thursday, and Sunday night for the past couple of years, I have given her one excuse or the other.

But last week, after getting back from Patrick's with Iris and Brian, I had been thinking about it a lot. I had turned down her invitations on Tuesday and Thursday nights, but yesterday I had found myself saying yes.

I remember the pause on her end as I had said I will come over for dinner. And then she had asked again, and I had repeated my confirmation.

Now, I can give her credit for her composure during the phone call, but I know how happy she is about me coming.

My heart sinks at the thought of having to take away that joy on her face. But having the flashback to that night many years ago suddenly makes me want to get out of the house immediately. The house seems to be closing in on me, and I suddenly find it hard to breathe.

My mom's face furrows in concern. She stretches her hand toward me.

"Son? Are you okay?" she asks.

I look at her, only at her, to steady myself. When I'm sure I can find my voice, I nod.

"I'm fine. But, I have to go. I'm sorry, something's come up at the office," I say.

I look into her eyes and see the knowledge of my bullshit in them. Alongside saddening disappointment.

I'm sorry, that's all I have, I think.

I lean in and kiss her cheeks. She blinks twice, surprised.

I'm surprised that I can give her that much too.

I turn back toward the door and open it, walking outside.

I get into my car and turn on the ignition. The memory of Iris and I standing in the foyer the night of my dad's birthday flashes into my mind.

I look at the house behind me in my rearview mirror. I guess it's now a place of both sad and happy memories.

It sure beats only sad memories, I think to myself as I drive off.

Chapter Twenty-Seven

Iris

I place the plate of sea bass on the table and look around the other dishes already arranged on it. A bowl of basmati rice, another bowl of baked potatoes, a plate of freshly baked bread, and a bowl of steamed vegetables.

I place the last dish, a bowl of salad, on the dining table, and then I look down at the spread.

I chew on the side of my lip as an uneasy feeling starts to spread within me.

"What are you doing, Iris?" I mutter to myself.

I know I'm doing a good thing, being thoughtful and considerate, and that's not a problem. The hitch is in how Dayton would react to this.

"He could be having a really crappy day, and he may just want to be alone," I reason with myself.

Because I know I sure feel that way sometimes.

I start tapping my foot incessantly as the uneasy feeling grows within me.

I look at the lit candles on the table. They illuminate the spread of food and give the room an intimate feel.

"The candles are probably too much. I mean, come on, Iris," I admonish myself.

I close my eyes, all at once annoyed with myself.

I have a reason for doing this, a damn good reason. Ever since Dayton had the dinner with his parents, he's been withdrawn. And having experienced the heart-wrenching distance between him and his parents first hand, I know something must have gone wrong.

And although we are more now to each other than we were when we started out, Dayton probably still doesn't feel connected enough with me to talk about it with me.

I glance toward Dayton's closed bedroom door, where the framed photograph of Melissa hangs.

And the memory of Dayton and I in the gazebo follows.

My musings are interrupted, and I glance toward the entrance of the house as the elevator makes a clicking sound and opens. Dayton walks out of it.

My heart starts to pound, and I wring my fingers together, suddenly nervous. I place a smile on my face, but even I can feel it tremble on my lips.

His steps falter as he notices my presence. He looks up at me, his eyes connecting with mine from across the room.

My heart pounds even louder.

"Hey," I say.

"Hey," he returns.

He looks past me to the dining table, and I wait. Seconds tick by, heavy with silence.

He looks back at me.

"I'm sorry you had to ask Brian for a key," he says.

And I feel my heart settle, just like that.

I smile, feeling like a fog has been lifted from my face.

"It's fine. I shouldn't have one, we're not real," I say, looking into his eyes.

He starts to walk slowly toward me, his eyes on mine. He stops by the sofa in the living room, takes off his suit jacket, and places it on the arm of the sofa. He rolls up the sleeves of his white shirt, at the same time loosening the button at the base of his neck.

And I know I have never seen a sexier sight.

He walks toward me and stands in front of me. He glances at the dining table, and then back at me.

"Thank you," he says.

I smile up at him. "You're welcome."

He is now in the kitchen area with me, and only the light from the candles illuminate here. The candlelight reflects over his face, and my heart clutches at the weariness I see in his eyes. All over his face.

I can't seem to look away from his gray eyes. I watch his gaze trail downward from my eyes. To my lips.

He grinds his teeth like he's trying to restrain himself. And that's what snaps me out of my stupor.

He told me he cared for me under the gazebo outside Patrick's home. He is happy to see me in his house, and he's not mad I got the key from Brian. He appreciates my food, and presence, tonight.

That might just be enough for me to take away the sad look in his eyes.

I place a hand on his arm and pull him gently toward a chair at the dining table. He sits, and I take the chair across from him.

His eyebrows jack up as he looks at the spread before him.

"You cooked all this?" he asks, a suspicious twinge in his voice.

I cock my head slightly to the side.

"You don't actually expect me to answer that, do you?" I ask back, a sly smile on my lips.

His lips quirk at the corners of his mouth, and even though the smile doesn't quite reach his eyes still, I feel happiness spread through me.

He takes up his fork and takes a cut from the sea bass, eats it. Takes a spoonful of basmati rice and another spoonful of salad.

And I watch him eat silently as I pick at my food.

"I never had dinner with my parents," he says suddenly.

My hand pauses with my fork halfway to my mouth. I place it down on my plate and stare at Dayton's bent head.

He finally looks up at me, directly into my eyes.

I don't say anything. I understand he is ready to talk, and for me to listen.

"I left," he continues. "I had a flashback to when I was seven when I entered the house." He pauses. "Maybe I matter now, but there was a time I didn't matter as much. And there's just something, just...something, stopping me from accepting that as it is."

His fist balls on top of the table. And my heart bleeds as I stare at a strong, powerful man, and I watch as he struggles with coming to terms with his level of importance to those who were supposed to love him the most.

I place my hand on top of his balled fist. He looks at the contact for a while, and then he lifts his eyes up to mine.

And I see what he needs in them.

I stand up slowly from my chair, my eyes never leaving his. I walk around to his side of the table.

My mind goes back to earlier, when he never corrected my statement about us not being real. But then again, the memory of us in the gazebo at Patrick's house flashes through my mind again. And how he said he cares about me.

"I care about you," I say to him now.

I frame his face in my hands, and I think to myself what I cannot say to him.

I want so much more from you. I want us to be real, and I want to be able to say so much more to you.

I smile at him as I lower my lips to his. As our lips touch, I close my eyes all the more to feel the kiss.

We stay like this, kissing, for a minute. And then Dayton slowly stands up from his chair. Our eyes on each other's, Dayton takes my hand and leads me to the bedroom.

"Iris," he whispers my name just before he lowers his lips to mine again.

I wind my hands around his neck, and he pulls me in closer to him. Where it had been fast and wild before with us, this is now slow and intentional.

I slowly pop the buttons on Dayton's shirt open. One by one till I remove the shirt and run my hands over the expanse of his chest. I look up into his eyes and frame his face with my hands.

"Like it was our first time, let me be the one to take away the pain this time. Let me do this for you," I whisper to him.

I lower my lips to his bare chest; I place kisses softly all over, stopping at his heart.

"Iris," he whispers my name again.

And it ends on a broken sigh.

"You undo me," he whispers as he places a kiss on my forehead.

I close my eyes, my heart filling and overflowing with emotions. Emotions so tender, I feel like I might break any second now.

My mind goes back to the first time we were together. Tonight is just like that night, I suddenly realize. No music, no seduction, just two hearts giving and taking.

Dayton peels my silk shirt away from my shoulders, and I feel heat pool at the base of my stomach. A slow burn gradually fills me, and I feel it at the tip of my fingers and down to my toes.

I throw my head back, giving Dayton more access as he lowers his lips to my shoulder blades.

He feasts on there for a minute, his hands roaming down till they get to the waistband of my jeans. He draws down the zipper, and I wiggle my hips slightly to let them slide down my legs.

He lifts his head up from my neck, and his eyes are black with desire as they stare at me. My pulse answers with a jerky quickening of its own.

I remove my legs from my jeans completely, kicking them away. I move closer to Dayton, unbuttoning his trousers. The pants slide down the length of his legs, and he also kicks them away.

I stand in front of him, my eyes on his, in my bra and panties.

Dayton's breath starts to come in hard, fast pants as he looks his fill.

"I need you," he says, his voice gravelly.

My heart pounds loudly in my chest, my body reacting to the naked desire in his voice. The heat in his eyes warms me from head to toe.

Slowly, he pulls me to the bed, laying me softly on the duvet. He joins me, kissing me. On my lips, down to my neck, to my breasts. My breath hitches as he gets to my stomach.

I feel his breath on my sex through my panties. I throw my head back as sensations slam into me.

"Dayton," I whisper, gripping the sheets to anchor myself.

"So beautiful," Dayton whispers as he stares at my lace panties.

He looks up at me, and my heart trips at the look in his eyes. Heat, yes, but also something else. Something deeper.

He bends down again and slowly removes my panties.

I hear him groan as his fingers brush against my wet folds.

Bright, explosive colors burst behind my eyes as the first finger sinks into my warmth.

"Ah!" I arch upward, toward the pleasure. "Dayton," I whisper.

"Think of me, only me," Dayton says as he continues to wreck me with his finger.

I look down at him, making sure my eyes are steady on his.

"Only you, Dayton. Only you," I say.

And then the pleasure builds up inside me, going so high as his fingers pound into me with skill and ferocity.

My eyes remain on his as the orgasm racks through my body.

As the shakes and vibrations in my body slow down to an ebb, I draw Dayton up to me and kiss him.

"Make love to me," I whisper to him.

Our eyes meet and emotions pass through his eyes, emotions that I know mean more than a care.

He asks the silent question of whether I am still on the pill. I nod my head, and he positions himself over me.

He slides into me, and our eyes remain on each other's as we start to move in tandem. His eyes darken even more as I clench around him, my wet folds sucking him in.

And the feeling of his orgasm racking through his body pushes me over the edge again. We come together.

Dayton lays on top of me, breathing heavily into my neck. I close my eyes and stroke his hair as a powerful wave of emotion runs through me.

I open my eyes and look up at the portrait of the smiling woman.

I love him.

CHAPTER TWENTY-EIGHT

Dayton

DAYTON

I squint my eyes against the rays of sun spilling into the room
through the blinds. I blink against it, finally opening my eyes fully.
I stay as I am for a minute, and then I turn my head to my other side.
And I see her.

Iris is laying on her back, her face turned toward me. Her hair
spills all over the pillow, fanning out in silky waves. Her brows furrow
slightly between her closed eyes like she's not satisfied about something in her sleep.

I feel my lips curve at that.

My mind flashes back to the first night we met, on the roof. Eyes
sparking with temper, mass tumble of full and rich black hair dripping
with drops of rainwater, and that cocksure stance.

What am I going to do with you? I think to myself. *What am I going to do with this need for you? This burning, helpless need for you.*

I close my eyes for a bit, and then I open them and stare right into black eyes.

"Hey," she says, a small smile curving her lips. Her eyes glint with the smile, and the sunlight streaming in meets it, sparking it.

My throat suddenly becomes dry. I try for a small smile.

"Hey back," I say, and then clear my throat when my voice comes out sounding scratched.

She smiles fully, and I feel my heart thud hard against my chest.

"What?" Iris asks.

And I realize I've been staring at her. I blink and smile at her.

"Nothing. Just thinking about your sea bass last night," I say.

"And?" she asks when I say nothing else.

My tongue in cheek, I look at her. "There was a little too much salt in it," I say.

It takes only an instant—her eyes widen in shock.

"You!"

And she starts attacking me with a pillow.

I laugh as I try to dodge the assault, and Iris pins me underneath her with both her legs on either side of me. Her hair tumbles around her and frames her face.

"You're dead," she says, looking down at me.

And proceeds to launch her attack on my face with the pillow. I allow it for a minute, listening to her laughter above me. And then I grip both her arms with my hands and pivot sharply till our positions are reversed. And she's pinned underneath me.

And as I look into her laughing eyes, I realize this position is not any better for my mental health.

"Accompany me to a party," I say suddenly.

The laughter slowly dies in her eyes as we stare at each other.

"Okay," she says simply.

We remain this way for a while, me staring down into her eyes, she staring up into mine.

Just this one day, I think to myself. *Just give me this one day.*

***

Later that night, 9 p.m., Iris walks out of her apartment building and toward me.

She is wearing a long, sequin, silver gown with a slit at the side up to her thigh. The gown hugs her figure, and the creamy skin of her thigh exposes just a little with every step she takes.

Her hair is piled atop her head in a messy bun, leaving tendrils of hair falling down around her face.

"So, what exactly is this party?" she asks as she stops in front of me.

"An engagement party," I say and walk toward the passenger side.

I open the door and look toward her, waiting for her to come around.

She walks over to the passenger side and, with a last smile at me, gets into the car.

I walk around to the driver's side and get in too.

"An engagement party. Anyone I know?" Iris asks.

I turn on the ignition and look into the rearview mirror before pulling out onto the road.

"It's an engagement anniversary actually. And yes, you know them." I pause and look over at her. "Katie and Alex," I say.

Iris's eyes widen. "For real?"

I nod.

Iris smiles. "Nice. How many years?"

"Ten."

Her eyes widen even more than before as she snaps her head toward me.

"Ten?! They've been together *ten years*?" she asks in shock.

I laugh. "Yeah. We have some that last, even in New York," I say with a sly smile.

Iris scoffs. "Of course I know that. It's just so rare," she says.

I laugh again. "I get you. They amaze me every time too," I say.

We both don't say anything for a while as I drive in silence.

And then suddenly, quietly, Iris says, "They still both look so happy."

I glance at her; her face is turned toward the sights outside the car window. A small, wistful smile is on her face.

My heart twists in my chest, and I grip the steering wheel tightly.

"They don't have children, you know," I say.

Iris turns her head to look at me.

"Really?"

I nod. "They both agreed to no kids, and they're apparently still happy about it."

"Wow," Iris says. She turns back to staring out the window. "I could never be satisfied with that though." She smiles, wistfully again. "I want kids, at least two of them," she says.

My heart twists painfully in my chest. I grip the steering wheel tightly again.

"I know," I say.

Iris turns to look at me. "You do?" she asks.

I nod.

I continue to look at the road ahead of me, but I feel Iris's gaze as she stares at me.

She must have seen something on my face, from my expression, because she sighs. She turns back to staring out the window.

"You do," she says, a little bit sadly.

My throat works as I swallow. My heart sinks knowing we just had an unsaid conversation that leaves us at an impasse.

We drive the rest of the way in silence.

Few minutes later, I pull up in front of the venue. I turn off the ignition, and we both get out of the car.

Loud music pounds out of speakers and outside.

Iris turns to look at me, her eyebrows raised. "It's not a quiet, dignified affair, is it?"

I smile. "No, it isn't," I say.

Iris smiles too. "I like Katie and Alex. They're good people."

I turn to face her; I place both hands on her arms and turn her to face me. I slide my hands down to hold both her hands in mine. She looks up at me.

"And because they are, let's have fun tonight. Just for tonight," I say.

Iris stares right into my eyes; she smiles.

"Yes, let's," she says.

I release one of her hands, and with the other still in mine, we enter the hall.

Over the course of the night, we mingle. Iris stays beside me the whole time I have a conversation with the head of a company I've been looking to acquire for a long time. And surprisingly, she even contributes. The company is a construction company.

"Didn't know you knew so much about concrete," I say to her once the CEO leaves.

She cocks her head slightly to the side, a teasing glint in her eyes.

"I have many layers," she says playfully.

"Yeah, I'm starting to see that," I say looking into her eyes.

We stare into each other's eyes, the party fading to the background.

And then the MC's voice in the microphone dispels the moment.

We mingle some more, sometimes with business associates of mine, sometimes with people from the fashion world.

Like Lisa Marion's cousin, Grace Underwood. She gushes over Iris's dress, impressed with it. We also meet Marie Ferrell, a senior designer who works at my fashion company, VIVID. Iris is apparently star struck as stares at the woman. And I remember her saying Marie is one of her idols in the fashion world.

"Grace says this gown is an original," Marie says as she studies the gown Iris is wearing.

Iris almost bobs her head. "Yes, it is," she confirms.

"Very impressive," she says before leaving.

Iris turns to me, her eyes wide with happiness.

"She said my gown is 'impressive,' my *work* is impressive. Oh my God! Did you hear that?"

I smile at her; her happiness is infectious. "I heard," I say.

She lets out a happy squeal.

Just then, Katie and Alex walk up to us. Twin smiles are on their faces, and they are obviously happy. Alex has his arm around Katie's shoulders, and Katie's hand covers his where it drops around her neck.

I feel a twinge of envy as I look at them.

"Hey guys!" Katie greets us.

"Having fun?" Alex asks.

"Very much," Iris says. "Congratulations, you two."

"Thank you," Katie replies, beaming. She looks between us and smiles. "You guys make such a beautiful couple. I love to see it."

I look down at Iris, she looks up at me.

Just then, "This Love" by Taylor Swift comes on through the speakers.

"Oh!" Katie suddenly exclaims and looks up at Alex. They both smile, obviously sharing a private joke.

Alex smiles at us as he takes his wife's hand.

"See you guys later, my love and I have an appointment on the dancefloor," he says and pulls Katie with him to the dancefloor.

As they leave, I turn to Iris and put out my hand.

"Come on," I say. "They obviously have a story behind this song. Let's create ours."

Iris's face slowly blooms till it fledges into a full smile.

She places her hand on mine, and we walk toward the dancefloor. I wrap my arm around her waist, pulling her toward me. She comes into my arms willingly and places her hand in mine.

She lays her head on my chest, and we start swaying slowly to the music.

We stay this way for a while, just swaying.

"Today has been magical," Iris suddenly whispers to me.

My heart clutches in my chest, my arms wrapping around her more tightly.

Iris sighs and closes her eyes.

"I don't ever want it to end," she says.

"Then we'll just stay this way," I say.

And we continue to sway slowly to the music.

***

Two hours later, I pull up in front of Iris's apartment building.

I twist my hand around the steering wheel, and my heart squeezes so painfully with the thought of what I have to do next, I think I might die from it.

Iris turns to look at me, a smile on her face. I don't turn to look at her because the sight of it would just be too much and might be the final twist of the knife currently in my heart.

"You want to come up?" she asks.

I swallow. "No," I say coldly.

There is silence for a beat.

And then, "Okay," Iris says slowly and a little too quietly.

I still don't look at her, but I know she's staring at me, trying to figure out what's wrong.

And in the silence, I say the words.

"We're over," I say simply.

There is silence again, this one so loud it pounds in my head.

"What?" Iris's voice cracks on the word.

I stare ahead. "Our agreement is up. Karen will send over a contract to you tomorrow to dissolve you of our earlier contract." My voice is cold, and my words precise and sharp. "I don't need you anymore, and I would like to draw the end of the line here."

I make myself turn to look at her. She is staring at the dashboard in front of her, a dazed look on her face, obviously not seeing anything.

I swallow. "You have been an efficient partner, and I thank you for your cooperation."

There is stunned silence from Iris as she continues to stare at the dashboard.

And then she opens the door and climbs out of the car.

I close my eyes on the slam of the door.

CHAPTER TWENTY-NINE

Iris

I stare at the wall in front of me, or more accurately, into space.

I feel dead inside, numb, cold, blank like the wall in front of me. I feel like I've been dragged by my morose shadow for the past month, and while the weight of it is heavy, I can't seem to put it down either.

I sigh—even I know I'm depressing myself. It's like I'm stuck in limbo, and I don't know how to get out of it. Ever since that day a month and two days ago, I have existed.

I go to work, return home, sometimes even have the strength to stand after-work drinks with friends. I've been able to do routine things, mundane activities, but never anything more than I have to do.

Why? This is the single question that keeps circling through my mind.

And it kills me, just kills me, every day, that I didn't ask the question that day.

"Why didn't I ask why?" I mutter to myself.

At the very least, I deserved an answer to a *'Why?'* question.

I run a hand through my hair and look up from my desk just as Alyssa walks up to me.

Her forehead mars with concern as she looks at me.

"Hey," she says.

I try a small smile. "Hey," I say back.

"Okay, so, don't freak out, but Lisa wants to see you." Alyssa pauses. "Big Lisa," she adds.

I feel a thud in my chest. I look around the office; no one else is around besides me and Alyssa. I look up at her.

"Six months ago, all I've ever wanted to hear were those words. Why am I not ecstatic?" I ask.

Alyssa crouches down till she's face to face with me.

"You are, in a part of you. The part of you that has wanted this ever since you moved here. That part is still in you, and it still wants it. You are just sad right now." She takes both my hands in hers and smiles at me.

I smile back, grateful for a friend like her.

"Now go stretch those designer arms," Alyssa says and stands up.

I stand up too and walk toward the elevator. I get in and the press the number for the top floor. As the doors slide closed, I take a deep breath.

"This is your career, Iris. Like Alyssa said, this is what you've been working toward for years now. This is it."

I take another deep breath as the elevator doors slide open again. I paste a smile on my face as I walk toward the receptionist's desk.

"Hi, Lorraine," I say, greeting the redhead at the desk.

She looks up and smiles at me. "Hey, Iris. Lisa is on a call right now, but she'll soon be done. Please wait a minute."

"No problem," I reply.

I shift a little to the side so I'm not in the way.

"So, heard you are dating Dayton Pade," Lorraine says.

I look at her, and I find her staring up at me with dreamy eyes.

She sighs. "God, what I wouldn't do to have a stud like that for a boyfriend." She twists her lips into a distasteful curl. "But all I manage to get are the frogs."

She sighs again and looks at me. Her face lights up in a smile as she stares at me. "I watched you guys interview with DISH. I just love the way he supports you and is so obviously proud of your achievements. Now, that's a man." Lorraine nods her head, obviously very convinced of her point.

I smile at her and choose to not say anything. Even as my heart is bleeding all over her desk.

Lorraine doesn't seem to notice either as she gushes on.

"Your life must be so full right now. You have a man that is the ultimate. You had your first fashion show, and it was successful. And the two go hand in hand so smoothly because you are dating a man. A real man. One who is not intimidated by your success."

Just then, Lisa's voice comes on over the intercom.

"Send her in."

Before Lorraine can turn to me to relate the message, I am already walking toward Lisa's doors.

Thirty minutes later, I walk out, dazed. I have a vague sound of Lorraine calling to me, but I don't even register it. I walk past her desk toward the elevator. I get in and get out as the doors open later on my floor.

I walk to the office I share with Alyssa and the other junior de-signers. I find Alyssa at her desk, her head bent over as she studies an ENAMORED fashion catalogue.

She looks up at me just as I get to her desk. Her gaze zeroes in on my face as she sees my expression.

"What happened? What's wrong?"

She stands up as she talks, and I drop into her chair. Alyssa crouches down like before again.

"Iris," she shakes me a little.

"My designs went farther than they expected," I say, my voice sounding like it's coming from far away.

"Than who expected?" Alyssa asks.

"Lisa and the board. She said my designs were widely voted as the best all across ENAMORED's other branches. All of them voted in favor of. All of them, Alyssa," I repeat, still dazed.

Alyssa's face lights up with happiness.

"Whoo! Damn right they voted in favor of," she says confidently.

I chuckle a bit, and I'm surprised I even can.

"They want to feature my designs in *Vogue*, Alyssa," I say.

Alyssa suddenly goes still. Her eyes widen.

"What?"

I nod my head, understanding her reaction perfectly. I feel like I'm in another world right now, and it's not real.

And then Alyssa suddenly screams.

I wince a little at the high pitch, and Alyssa just keeps on saying 'oh shit' over and over again.

I close my eyes and rub my hand over my heart. The pain that has been lodged there over the past few weeks is even more pronounced now.

I want to tell Dayton, I realize. I want to call him right now and tell him all about it. I want to scream and react the way Alyssa is doing now, with him.

I rub a hand over my chest again and stand up.

"I have to go," I mutter.

"What?" Alyssa turns to me, still riding the good news high.

"I need to walk, get some fresh air," I say.

Alyssa looks at my face more closely, and concern mars her face again.

"Do you want me to come with?" she asks.

I smile at her. "No, I'm good. I just need to be alone for a while," I say. "Thanks," I add before taking my jacket from the back of my chair and walking out.

I walk out of ENAMORED's front door and out to the street.

I turn right and start walking. As I pass Enzo's food truck, my heart twists painfully in my chest remembering when Dayton and I had eaten there together.

I wave at Enzo and continue walking. Few minutes later, I come upon Prospect Park. I branch in, the calm atmosphere drawing me in.

A few people mill about, most of them just wandering about and enjoying the afternoon breeze. I walk over to the pier overlooking the stream.

I lean against the rails and look out at the stretch of water. I take a deep breath in, closing my eyes.

Alyssa's words from earlier, when I had asked her why I was not ecstatic about Lisa wanting to see me, come back to me.

You are, in a part of you. The part of you that has wanted this ever since you moved here. That part is still in you, and it still wants it. You are just sad right now.

"I am just sad right now," I mutter to myself.

Alyssa had said it like it was okay to be sad. And maybe it is. But why don't I feel okay with it?

Because I don't want to be sad anymore, I realize.

The faint afternoon breeze blows by, and my eye catches a woman a few feet away from me. She's painting on an easel; her bright yellow scarf billows around her neck in the wind. A little boy munches on his cotton candy a few feet away from the artist, as his mother drags him along. Two teenage girls giggle as they walk past me.

I want to be happy again, I realize. I want to be able to giggle at something funny. I want to munch on cotton candy and enjoy it.

And I want to design again, I think to myself as my eyes go back to the woman painting on her easel.

My designs are going to be in *Vogue*, and I want to be damn happy about it.

I take a deep breath again, and this one doesn't come with pain.

CHAPTER THIRTY

Dayton & Iris

Dayton

I adjust the collar of my shirt beneath my suit. I don't know why I feel irritated, I just do.

Maybe it's the heat. I look around my office. Did the AC stop working? My gaze zeroes in on the AC in the corner of the room. I snarl at the quiet humming sound it makes as it works perfectly.

So it's not the AC then.

I look down at the party flier on my desk. The launch party for the new tech company, TECHED, that I just acquired last week is happening tonight. It's going on right now on the roof above my head.

The hand in my hair goes down to the back of my neck, and I start to rub there. Lately, I feel like my whole body is on pins and needles, and I ache all over.

The past month has been hell. Hell like I have never known before. Drowning myself in work leaves me exhausted, and when it comes time to rest at night, sleep eludes me.

I walk over to a glass table in one corner of my office. I take the bottle of whiskey on it and pour into a glass cup. I take a sip and let the warm liquid swirl in me.

I walk over to the glass wall where the street of New York stretches out before me. I stand and watch as cars and people drive and walk past respectively.

The city that never sleeps, I think to myself. I feel that now more than ever, except I'm not brimming with energy like the city. I'm just numb.

And angry, and miserable.

I raise my glass of whiskey to my lips and slowly bring it back down. My heart starts to pound as my eyes fix on Iris down on the curb in front of the building.

***

IRIS

"No, no, no, no, what are we doing here?" I turn to Brian, then turn back to look up at Dayton's office building. "Brian, no. What are we doing here? I can't be here."

I start to walk away, my heart pounding loudly in my chest. I hadn't been looking at where we were going while the taxi that just dropped us off drove us down here.

I really hadn't been able to bring myself to care about where Brian had insisted that he had to suddenly take me to when he had come over to my house earlier. But now that I see where it is, I care. I care very much.

"I can't be here," I mutter to myself.

Brian's hand on my arm halts my hasty retreat.

I look up at him, into his warm brown eyes, and I'm suddenly scared. I'm suddenly scared that he will convince me to talk to Dayton. Because if anybody can, it's Brian.

"Please don't make me talk to him," I plead with Brian.

I suddenly feel tears prick at the back of my eyes.

Brian's face dissolves into warm concern. He runs both his hands up and down my arms, pulling me closer to him.

He lifts my head with a finger. "You have to talk to him," he says, his voice gentle.

I shake my head; Brian's hands just remain firm.

"Yes, you do. He's leaving," he adds.

And shock holds me still as the implication of Brian's words hit me. I look into his eyes, and my heart sinks.

Almost afraid to ask, I swallow. "When?" I ask anyway.

"The day after tomorrow," Brian says.

I swallow again.

"You need to talk to him. And he needs to talk to you. You both need to listen."

I look up at Brian and nod slowly. Brian smiles a little and takes my hand in his. We walk toward the building's entrance.

We walk toward the elevator and get in. Few minutes later, the doors slide open, revealing a party in full swing.

Overhead light garlands twinkle above our heads as Brian and I walk into the party. People mill about and mingle, champagne flutes in their hands. A live band plays softly on their instruments, and the music matches the sophisticated mood of the party. Glasses clink against each other in toasts.

Of their own volition, my eyes are drawn to the railing surrounding the roof. A memory of me screaming at the sky and the busy street of New York about my asshole of a boyfriend, one night roughly six months ago, flashes through my mind.

And my lips curve at the memory. Carl Lingstrom. *Barely a blip on my radar now*, I think to myself.

And then I remember seeing Dayton for the first time. His face, as the lightning that had accompanied the rain that night streaked across it. The punch I had felt in my stomach at the sight of the beauty, the poise and power as Dayton had stood in front of me.

I turn away from the railing and hold a hand to my stomach. My stomach is in knots just thinking about it.

I turn to tell Brian I can't do this, I can't see Dayton. And I find myself looking into Dayton's eyes.

My hands tighten on my stomach as I feel that punch again. Only this time in threefold.

A painful feeling squeezes my chest tightly as I stare up into Dayton's face. I hurt, I hurt so bad just looking at his face. And yet I can't seem to look away.

I swallow deeply. "Dayton." It's barely a whisper.

Even his name threatens to choke me. I clear my throat.

"Iris," he says.

My whole body responds to his voice, and I ache with the loneliness that had become a part of me for the past month.

As I open my mouth to talk, the skies open up and rain starts to pour down in sudden and heavy droplets.

The party guests start to rush toward the roof entrance amid squeals and shocked exclamations. The band scrambles to pack up their instruments, and I see Brian help one of the members, a woman, with her violin.

Dayton grabs my hand and starts to pull me away toward the entrance too. I dig in my heels, rooting myself to the spot.

Dayton glances back at me, his hair dripping with rainwater.

"What are you doing? Let's get out of the rain!" he shouts to be heard above the sound of the rain.

"No," I say.

Dayton stares at me in disbelief. "What?" he asks incredulously.

I don't know why I suddenly feel strongly about remaining on the roof. Then again, I think back to the first night I had come up to this roof to vent out my anger. Yes, it had been anger at Carl and his asshole behavior toward me, but it had also been pain. I had also been feeling hurt, and I had come up to this roof to make myself feel better.

So I remember that first night, on this same roof, the rain falling just like now, lightning streaking across Dayton's face like it just did now. And I think maybe I know why I feel strongly about remaining on the roof. Because just like that first night, I'm hurting tonight too.

"You're leaving?" I ask Dayton.

He stares at me, frustration warring with bafflement, and resignation finally winning.

"Yes," he says.

I swallow. The rain continues to pound over us.

"Why?" I ask. Before Dayton can reply, I clarify, "Not why are you leaving? Why did you end us?"

"Because I can't give you what you want," Dayton says with hesitation.

I turn to look at him slowly. "And what is that?"

Dayton runs a hand through his hair, and my heart clutches at the motion.

"A family," he bites out. His voice is harsh and bitter now, and his face resonates anger. He balls his fist at his side. "A husband, kids, a home. I can't give you any of it," he says.

My heart starts to pound in my chest, and I realize there is a storm brewing inside of me.

I ball my fist too. "And you know I want this, how?" I ask quietly.

He turns to face me. "You said so. That night, in the car, on the way to Katie and Alex's party."

I snap my face toward him, and I'm sure my eyes are sparking with my anger.

"I said I could never be satisfied with not having kids! I never said anything about *you* giving me kids!" I shout, suddenly so angry at him.

Confusion runs across Dayton's face for a second.

I take a deep breath. "So, you broke up with me, ended things between us—something really great that was going on between us—without any explanation, for that?"

Dayton stares at me for a second, and then he explodes.

"Yes, I did! Okay? Yes, I did. And even though it's not a problem right now, don't stand there and tell me it's not going to be a problem down the line. I see myself spending the rest of my life with you, and the issue of having or not having kids is inevitable."

He stops and runs a hand through his hair again, frustration and anger clearly vibrating through him. He turns away from me to pace.

"You saw my family, the house I grew up in. The party that night? Those were the kind of parties I grew up in. I was invincible, and I never mattered enough to make time for." He stops pacing, and his shoulders drop as if in defeat. His voice is quiet as he talks now, and my heart twinges at the sadness in his words. "I can't do that to another kid," he says.

I remain where I am for another minute. And then I start to walk toward him. As I get a step away from him, he speaks up again.

"I took down Melissa's portrait," he says.

I stop walking. He turns to face me. The rain beats down on us. And I close the gap between our lips.

Warmth, pulsing heat, courses through my whole body even as the cold droplets of rain hit me. Dayton's hands come up to frame my face as he takes over the kiss, his tongue pushing against my tongue.

My lips tingle as we separate. Dayton's hands remain on my face, and my body hums like a heater turned on at the highest.

I look up into his eyes, and they are dark with desire and focused on me.

"I am not letting you go," I say. "You are never going to do to your kid what your parents did to you. I know this like I know my own name. And I am going to be there until you realize it yourself."

I raise my hands to frame his face too, making sure my eyes stay steady on his. "Kids are our future. You and I, we are right now. And we are great. So I'm not letting you go, ever again. Melissa loved you, and I will always be grateful to her for giving you her love. Just like I will give you mine now."

I watch Dayton's eyes widen slightly at my words, and I feel my heart take lift at the expression in them. I suddenly feel like laughing, so I smile instead.

"You deserve love, Dayton, because you have so much of it to give," I say.

His hands tighten on my face, and I watch as his throat moves as he swallows deeply.

"I don't see it as you do, yet," he says, his voice deep with emotion. "But I know one thing. I love you."

And I release the happy bubble in me. I laugh even as my eyes full with tears. I chuckle wetly.

"Took you long enough," I say.

Dayton smiles and leans down to kiss me again.

We separate again and I look into his eyes.

"Where are you going?" I ask, referring to him leaving.

"I have a business trip to Paris. It's for six months," he says.

A smile blooms on my face.

"What a coincidence. ENAMORED is sending me to Paris for fashion week as some of my designs will be used in the show. And they're sponsoring me for," I pause, smiling up at Dayton, "six months," I finish.

Dayton smiles down at me. "Damn fine coincidence," he says.

We both laugh.

"Guess we're going to Paris together," Dayton says.

I smile. "Guess we are," I confirm.

And I close my eyes as Dayton leans down to kiss me again. The rain continues to pour.

Perfect.

—

THE END

Did you like *Faking It With My Enemy*? Then you'll LOVE *Faking it With My Billionaire*.

Read *(Faking It With My Billionaire)* **Now**

This off limits age gap steamy romance will have you panting for more. Read chapter one on the very next page!

Sneak Peek

Faking It With My Billionaire Sneak Peak

My dress stuck to my body like a glove, making me slightly uncomfortable, and my huge quartz ring kept slipping down my finger.

"It was your grandmother's. She wanted you to have it," Dad had said when he slipped the ring onto my index finger earlier that evening.

"I guess I can see it now. The resemblance is uncanny. Who'd ever think that Arden and Olivia would find their long-lost daughter..."

"The new Monroe heiress? To me, it all seems too convenient that a full-grown woman is coming to claim the business that..."

I tuned the words out, trying to quieten the whispers that got louder by the minute. It was even worse that they were all directed at me. Each judgmental whisper I heard was coupled with quick glances in my direction and sometimes loud tutting.

I took a long sip of champagne, my eyes scanning the vast dining hall filled with at least a hundred people. I couldn't for the life of me understand why the New York elite thought it was a good idea to meet up every few months to boast about how many properties they had, or whose number was highest on the Forbes list, or the vacation house that Lauren Kim had snagged off the market. It baffled me all the more that I was now considered a part of the elite, and that singular notion sent a shiver throughout my body. I downed the remaining champagne, hoping the alcohol would quell my nervousness.

"Woah, easy there, tiger," said my cousin Miranda, taking away the full glass of champagne I'd grabbed off a waiter's tray.

"I can't just pretend they're not all gossiping loudly about me," I moaned.

"Well, that's one of the few horrors you'd have to face as being one of us."

"Us?" I questioned, a small smile playing on my lips.

"Goddamn it! *Them*. You know I meant them."

I giggled softly, relief washing over me. I was so glad that I'd met Miranda. Finding out I had a cousin my age and also one who was so down to earth had been precisely what I needed to navigate the crazy world I was thrown into. After her single mother died of leukemia, Miranda moved in with her aunt and uncle, who were my parents. She'd been like the daughter they'd lost until they found me a few weeks ago.

Growing up, I'd been a little bit curious about who my parents were, but I'd been tagged an orphan at the orphanage, so I never went out in search of them. When I got the call and met up with Dad, I was completely shocked by the news and all the pictorial evidence he showed.

I couldn't believe that my parents were actually alive and had been searching for me for years without giving up hope. I was even more shocked when I was told that I was the heiress of one of the biggest jewelry companies in the world.

For the longest time, I thought myself an orphan, but finding out I actually had a family that cared enough about me to consistently keep searching for years was all the validation I needed.

This New York elite ball was my debut into high society, as Miranda had said, and it was evident from the number of stares I was getting that I wasn't entirely welcome.

"Uh-oh," Miranda started. "Marino Dellucci at 12 o'clock."

"Who?" I asked, looking straight ahead at the flamboyantly dressed man approaching us.

"Don't tell me you don't know Marino." Miranda rolled her eyes at me.

"If I did know him, I wouldn't be asking you who he was, would I?" I asked through gritted teeth.

"Well, he's here already. Just smile and nod."

And instantly, Marino Dellucci was standing before us, all grace and poise. He wore a huge multicolored boubou, and his slicked-back hair was held back by at least a gallon of hair gel.

"*Amore mio*. You look even more ravishing than in the papers." He stepped back and gasped. "And your style, amazing!"

"The papers?" I shot a look at Miranda.

"Si. You've been all over them and even on the news. It's an honor." I was caught off guard as soon as he dipped his head, placed his right hand dramatically on his chest, and bowed.

"Oh," I chuckled nervously, pulling him up. "That's not necessary."

"I need to pay my reverence. You're the heiress of the Monroe Jewelry, and by now, I'm sure you're sick and tired of hearing just how great our parents are."

I was mainly sick and tired of being constantly reminded of how lucky I was to be the daughter of such elites—as if I had planned the whole thing myself. I was also not ignorant of the looks I was getting.

A twenty-five-year-old woman randomly fell into the New York elite scene. Sure, it does seem shady, but it wasn't like I had concocted it all in a basement somewhere. The DNA test came back positive, and that was enough proof.

Marino started talking again. "I should dress you for your next event. You would look absolutely wonderful."

I nodded shyly as he handed me his business card and sauntered away.

I turned to Miranda. "Um, what just happened?"

"Marino fucking Dellucci paid his reverence to you and also offered to style you." Miranda was practically hopping up and down beside me with a broad smile.

"And...is that a good thing?"

"That's the best thing, Hazel. Not only does it mean he likes you, but he also gave your dress a stamp of approval which means a lot in the fashion world."

I feigned a sigh of relief. "Wow, finally, someone who doesn't want to dump their top-shelf drink on me."

Miranda giggled and linked her arm with mine. "Come on; they're not all bad. They're just shocked that they have to acclimate themselves with someone who wasn't born into *the* society."

I rolled my eyes. "Imagine how I feel."

"Oh fuck!" Miranda said suddenly beside me. "Kelly Duval is here, and I need to follow up on a correspondence from work."

"Wait," a wave of panic crept into my voice. "Don't tell me you're leaving me all alone in this den of wolves?"

"Mingle, Hazel. That's how you survive the den of wolves. You make friends with the wolves," she said and hurried off to where a group of women stood, leaving me all alone.

I sighed and grabbed another drink from a passing waiter. Bringing it up to my lips, I relished the clean taste of the champagne.

The stares around me were more blatant now that Miranda, who'd been my social safety net, had left me all alone. I could hear the whispers picking up again, and it took everything in me not to scream.

What was the point in trying to mingle? I saw no point in getting prepared by an entire glam squad only to stand around in an insanely expensive dress, sipping a glass of equally expensive champagne and being judged. Transitioning from a small-town New York girl to the talk of the city was something I'd never envisioned even in a million years.

Fuck it. I'd been judged enough this evening to last me a lifetime.

I placed the almost-empty glass of champagne on a nearby table and turned toward the exit, when I saw my parents approaching. They were hand-in-hand, and the faces of those around who'd been staring daggers at me a few minutes ago were all in wide smiles.

My parents. The words felt foreign in my head. For twenty-five years, I'd never had the privilege of saying those words until a few weeks ago.

They were perfect. They were everything I'd ever imagined and more, and they were *my* parents. The smile on my face widened as they approached me.

Blending into the family and being cared for was by far the easiest part about the transition. It was so easy, too easy, to fall in love with these fantastic people. It was as if all my life, I'd been waiting to meet them, to love them how I'd always wanted to. And it happened; I met them, and loving was seamless, effortless.

"Hazel," mom cooed, pulling me into a bone-shattering hug as if she hadn't seen me just a few hours ago. She pulled back and examined me, letting out a soft gasp. "You look absolutely breathtaking."

"I got it from you," I responded with a smile.

I'd gotten her raven black hair which cascaded down both our backs, and her bright green eyes. She was a gorgeous woman, and when I met her for the first time, I could tell instantly that she was my mother. She'd started the jewelry business with Dad and was now an empire owner, professional socialite, and philanthropist. Dad, on the other hand, spent his off days—which was basically every day—playing golf with his friends.

"I had to wait for her to finish getting ready, which, as you know, already takes forever," Dad grumbled as mom swatted him playfully on the arm.

"After twenty-six years, one would think you would've gotten used to this by now, but all you do is complain."

"I could never complain about anything you do, my love."

He pulled her for a hug, the sight melting my heart. The love and romance they shared was another thing I'd missed out on, and after more than twenty-six years, they still looked at one another with so much love.

"Okay, you two should go around and mingle. I don't want to hoard you all night."

But that wasn't true. If I could have them all to myself forever, I would.

"We'll make the rounds and come keep you company, honey," Mom said, which was sweet but made me feel more miserable than I already felt.

"No, I'm perfectly fine on my own. You both can go hang out with friends."

Dad raised an eyebrow. "Really?"

"Yes, really. Now shoo."

Giving me quick hugs, they made their way to where their friends were.

My eyes scanned the room, looking for nothing in particular, when Miranda rushed toward me. "Oh my God, Hazel, he's here."

"Who?"

She ignored me and continued. "He never comes to these kinds of things because he's all high and mighty, but that's just Forrest, you know—New York City heartthrob. Gosh, I understand why now. My heart is beating so hard right now, and it's not stopping—"

I shook Miranda back to reality. "Who are you talking about?"

She blinked at me, her eyes glazed over as if she was only just seeing me.

"*Forrest Woods.*"

"Forrest Woods? Who's that?"

She rolled her eyes. "I can't believe how uninformed you are."

"I'm only informed about current affairs."

"Forrest Woods *is* current affairs."

"Just spit it out." I glared at her. "Who's this Forrest Woods?"

"The man currently holds the number seven position on the Forbes Billionaires list."

I shook my head. "Doesn't ring a bell."

"Woods Dermatology Company?"

"Still nothing."

Miranda groaned. "Anyway, he's one of the biggest billionaires in the game currently. His parents are or were family friends, but ever since they died, Forrest has just kept to himself."

I looked around the room filled with snooty women who wore rows and rows of pearls on their necks and men who spoke as if they had a watermelon stuck up their colons. No one in their right mind would willingly attend such an event.

"And he's here?"

"I know. I'm as shocked as you are."

It was the first time that evening that Miranda looked animated, and as I looked around the room, I heard whispers float around; and none of them were about me. Whoever this Forrest Woods was, he certainly seemed like a big deal.

I exhaled, feeling lighter than I'd been all night. "Finally, a new topic for the night that isn't about me."

"No offense, and I love you, Hazel, but I guarantee you that with Forrest here, no one is even thinking about you."

"Ha ha ha, thanks a bunch, Miranda."

"I was only telling the truth, though."

"Well, there are some truths that should—" Before I could finish speaking, Miranda cut me off with a low gasp, her fingernails digging into my skin.

"He's here."

The hall fell silent, and everyone, including myself, was holding their breath. I craned my neck to see what all the fuss was about, and my eyes caught a man with dark brown hair and extremely broad shoulders standing by the entrance. I sucked in my breath at the sight; his presence was magnetic.

He stood tall, scanning the crowd, his bright, smoldering blue eyes looking around the room in derision. And then his eyes landed on me, held mine, and I was instantly frozen to the spot.

A rush of awareness ran through my spine, and I was sure that whoever this man was, he'd be the death of me.

(Click here to get Faking It With My Billionaire)

Made in the USA
Monee, IL
02 July 2024